Rena, A Late Journey

Photo by John C. Andrews

Eve La Salle Caram

Plain View Press
P.O. 33311
Austin, TX 78764

512-441-2452
sbpvp@eden.com
http://www.eden.com/~sbpvp
1-800-878-3605

ISBN: 0-911051-20-1
Library of Congress Number: 99-066672
Copyright Eve La Salle Caram, 2000.
All Rights Reserved.

Books by Eve La Salle Caram

RENA, A Late Journey
PALM READINGS, Stories from Southern California (Editor)
WINTERSHINE
DEAR CORPUS CHRISTI
Available from Plain View Press.

Contents

The author also wishes to thank:
Susan Bright for editing;
Stel DeLeón for transcription;
Roberta Kanefsky, Sharron Kollmeyer
and Maria Elouina Kasilag for proof reading and special
assistance; and, as always, her daughter, Bethel Eve,
for her love and encouragement and for her creative spirit.

In memory of my Aunt Bo,
Leola Merritt Davitt,
and of all beloved departed.
With grateful acknowledgement (once again) to
The Corporation of Yaddo

"As a blind man, lifting a curtain, knows it is morning,
I know this change:
On one side of silence there is no smile;
But when I breathe with the birds,
The spirit of wrath becomes the spirit of blessing,
And the dead begin from their dark to sing in my sleep."

Theodore Roethke
-from *"Journey to the Interior"*

At the Seawall

Part One

Photo by Daryl Bright Andrews

The Last Dime Store

"Don't tell me Kress's is still here? Why, it must be the last dime store! And here I am seeing it in my last days."

That's what I said when I got off the bus for the last time there in Corpus Christi.

Now I don't have to be transported by bus. Like one of those gulls on the bay front. I just hover.

At that time, late in one of the last decades of the century, I was into my nineties, in good health, but a little unsteady. My nephew, Searcy, who lived in Nacogdoches and has always been nearby, argued with me about taking the bus trip from the Houston terminal. He didn't even seem to understand why I had to go.

I had to go because Leeland, my husband who wrote "I love you" on a pad for me to see just before he died (with cancer of the throat, he couldn't speak, honey), had come in a dream and told me, "Rena, go back to Corpus Christi one last time while you can still go fishing, while you can still get around. You'll enjoy it and maybe go on to something new there, something you need to find."

Then I asked, "What is it?" And wouldn't you know it? Once again he was mute.

But I knew I should listen to my dream. All my life dreams had been taking me places. I got into trouble when I didn't listen, didn't go.

When I was just seventeen and pregnant for my first and only time, I didn't go to see my mama who we called Mammy or my little sister, Lucy, who up until the time she died, was a healer (she couldn't heal herself, honey!) and that caused me to lose my baby. My dream told me to go back to Mammy and to try and find Lucy so the baby who I called Juliette — because she was beautiful as a girl in a play — would be safe. But I didn't; the husband I was with then made fun of me, said I was dumb like all women and superstitious like all Creoles, like all my family. Can you imagine that? When I was just a child, I married a man like that, stayed with a man like that? Oh, but not for long, darlin'.

This was years before I met Leeland, but even then I wasn't crazy.

After that when I dreamed, I tried to pay attention. If a dream told me to take a trip, not long after I was on the bus, on a train! And from childhood, right up until the last months of my life, was as blessed with health, with only a little tendency in my nineties to lose my balance and topple over. Even then I usually did all right on my three-pronged cane.

But in Corpus Christi I had forgotten about the wind which had a force and a character unlike any other. You would be wrong not to address it, not to speak to it as you would an entity, not to give it a proper name.

"You're one of the things I've forgotten," I told it out there on the street corner. "I would do all right in Corpus Christi if I hadn't forgotten you." I didn't believe there was anywhere on earth where the wind could blow like it does in South Texas there on the Coastal Bend.

Blows a constant gale that rocked the bus I was on as it drove along on that long, gray road, cotton fields stretched out either side on flat-flat land, telephone poles stringing out to the sky.

We followed the same two-lane highway we took years ago on that flat lowland —and oh, it was way low down, below sea level, scrubby green country covered with a big gray sky, green leaves from the cotton fields rippling. Green as they were because of a summer of unusual rain. Miles of Black-Eyed Susans alongside, all the way to a town called Beeville where no bee or anything else ever seemed to be buzzing, to the bleak towns of Sinton and Taft which seemed mostly concrete, mostly highway, and finally after miles more of flatland, low moving clouds over it, into a little crossroads of a town called Gregory which should have been named World's End — for there the end of the world seemed called for — and beyond it, Portland, overcast, but which did transport, for from it, coming down a little grade (some called it a hill, low down as we were), we could see some of the Gulf, then Corpus' little bay and above it, an ocean of sky, and just below that, the city.

High-rises right on the bay front shocked me. Years ago, only hotels on the bluff rose more than four or five stories. When I first came, Corpus Christi was only a few thousand people and seemed the sweetest little town sitting there on its bay so quietly. Well, now it's like everywhere. Oh, honey, the world is overbuilt and close to breaking.

When we made it over the Causeway and past North Beach on the bay side of us and the sign of *The Caller Times* building on the other, and what I used to think of as town, the first marked building I spotted was Kress's. (Oh, what a landscape I had been traveling over, telephone wires running messages and newspapers calling out the times!)

"Why, is Kress's still here?" I asked the bus driver. I had spent many hours of my lifetime in Kress's. And since the wind nearly knocked me over as soon as I stepped out of the bus station — leaning on my cane with all I had in me — I was happy to once again see that Kress's store!

I told myself I could buy a scarf in it and have a bite to eat and a cup of coffee if the lunch counter was still there, ask directions and get my balance. What had I meant coming without a scarf? I could consider that. Get all my thoughts together.

Nobody was on the street when I crossed, leaning into the wind on my cane without too much trouble. I had all I'd brought with me, medicines, a nightgown, cold cream and two changes of clothing, in a Foley's shopping bag I carried over one arm. I never believed in carrying much with me, talked Searcy out of using his valise.

Once I was inside Kress's, I found the scarves on a rack not far down the center aisle right away. Though red was always my color (and I liked a bright one with some gold shot through it), I had on a dark blue cotton — the red just too hot to look at the day I left so I stuck it in my Foley's bag — and I picked out a blue scarf to match, and also, for a change, a black one, the color some of my hair still was, to go with my pocketbook and shoes.

A Mexican boy with long eyelashes, wearing a shirt bright as cotton leaf, left the jewelry counter to sell it to me. "With a wind like you have in Corpus Christi," I told him, "these must be a popular item. All the tourists must buy them."

The boy said Corpus didn't have too many tourists and that because of the lack of jobs, his one sister, a few of his brothers and almost all of his cousins had left the county.

"Honey," I told him as I picked a loud pink scarf that caught my eye off the rack and handed him another two dollars, "if you have brothers and sisters who don't have jobs, sell them a bunch of these and send them out to get twice the price for them on the street corners."

The boy said he didn't think Corpus had too many buyers anywhere. "The wind," he said, waving an arm, "blows everybody and all the money right out of town." Then from the tag he was wearing on his shirt, I found out his name, RENATO, and it startled me, for I saw the first of my name in it. (I found out later he was part Italian on his mother's side.)

He reminded me of a boy, also Mexican Italian, I used to see with Elizabeth, Leeland's niece who I helped raise after her father took off and her mother went to work in another town. But that was years and years before. Maybe forty years had passed since I saw her talking with that boy right in Kress's. People said he went off to North Beach with sailors who bought him things. Now that boy would be a man.

"Renato," I asked, "do you have an older relative who used to work here?"

"At one time or another all my relatives have worked here," he told me, "but the pay is so bad that finally they all take off."

Not much I could do with that so I changed the subject. "Do they still make strawberry sundaes over at the lunch counter? With those good frozen berries? I always liked any kind of berry."

"Sure do," he said in a velvety voice, "and with whipped cream and a large cherry on top."

"What counties did your brothers and one sister leave for, honey?"

"Webb and Maverick and Zavala, Uvalde and Medina, counties all over South and Central Texas," he told me. "My twin brother, Reynaldo, left before he finished high school after our mother passed away. And then my sister, Mara, got married and moved to San Antonio. But Jesus has not left yet and he is the oldest, and my baby brother, Julio, is still here. We have cousins who have moved everywhere, I'll bet you all over Texas and all over the United States. Some to cold places like Kansas City. But we don't hear from nobody so I don't know how they are doing or even where most of them are."

"You have a large family," I told him, "so it's easy to lose track." I had tied the black scarf around the back of my head the way the nuns taught me when I was a girl in their school in Louisiana, and I dropped my other scarves in a shopping bag. When I caught my reflection in the lunch counter mirror a little later, I saw the scarf made me look like an old nun.

"Scattered to the winds now," he said and pointed to the street which I knew had no one much on it.

For I had just walked a ghost street, no longer the main drag. Chaparral only ran three or four blocks, the Central movie house across from Lichtenstein's Department Store which I had been told was closed (and later its windows all boarded up) on one end of it, and the Ritz, where the Bells saw all those Bette Davis shows they liked so much on the other.

When I crossed that street I noticed Kress's was one of the few streets still open for business. And for all I knew, the wind that was still blowing a gale would one day blow poor jobless Renato right out of town as it had done the rest of his kin. I saw when I crossed Chaparral that the Ritz had a sign that said CLOSED FOREVER on the front door, the criss-crossed plastic strips on the marquee broken and peeling and flapping in the wind.

I remembered Ellen Bell, Leeland's mother, saying, "People in Corpus Christi walk around with their heads tied up in rags." A good thing I had bought several. Oh, on that day I was glad to have the scarves from Renato! I would try to get a city bus to the Ramada Inn which was only a few blocks away. Not that it was my idea of a place to stay. Still a room would be comfortable there, I supposed, and in this new Corpus Christi, as good as any other.

My first idea when I talked about taking this trip with Searcy was to rent a room in the big old-fashioned rooming house that used to stand on the edge of the park just the other side of the Ritz picture show where Leeland and I once lived and were happy. Of course, it's no longer there.

I could still hear Leeland saying, "Rena, bring me my specks, I want to read you something." Then he picked the Bible up from the bridge table where he worked on plans for some buildings no one wanted to commission or construct.

What did he read that day? I think maybe it was just once again from the Easter story, the last of the book of Mark that he read so often. Outside I watched the azalea and the first canna blooming. I don't remember exactly where he began, only him reading about how Jesus, after he had risen from the dead, appeared first to Mary Magdalene. And how it was Mary M., as I always called her, — the M. for the fishing village where she had been born — who spread the news about seeing him. Seeing him and talking with him on the road, Leeland always emphasized that, that Jesus came to Mary M. on a road, like one in Texas he and his Daddy had helped turn into a highway. In the 30s they even worked on the one that swooped down from Portland to the Causeway and then C.C. Mary M. was the first of God's new messengers put on a road to spread heavenly news, a woman of the road, Leeland said, in a time when women didn't travel.

How in the springtime, every springtime, Leeland loved to read or tell that story — the only others he read us for fun in the evening, spy stories or Ellery Queen.

How much pleasure we enjoyed in that little room in the rooming house with the park on one side. A place where we had nothing. Not even a refrigerator or a stove, only a hot plate and a window cooler to keep snacks in. I kept the colored eggs there that I boiled and dyed every spring, bought the dye for them at Kress's. We ate them, one by one, and gobbled them down along with all that mystery of spring. (Darling, spring is the mystery season.) Our own home communion! We didn't need a church.

Leeland kept his strong cheeses in our cooler and I saved the pot liquor from the vegetables I boiled on the hot plate every noon. Oh, I always liked a good boiled lunch. We relied on that cooler to keep food fresh for us and trusted the Gulf gale to blow the stench from it away.

We rented the room which came furnished, so poor that we didn't even own the bed we slept and loved each other on. But we were happy. And often had a neighbor or two in, Myrna Teague who lived just below us, a widow, who liked to drink beer with us and smoke cigarettes and talk with Leeland — honey, they both died speechless with malignant tumors of the throat — and quilt sometimes with me. And the boy, Billy, who cleaned the park, picked up trash with a spiked stick, weak of mind and leg, but full of laughter — he couldn't remember his name, but I called him Billy Park — sometimes he came to visit, too.

And sometimes Leeland would read the paper to him, or maybe even some Bible stories about the miracles. He liked to dwell on those. Raising Lazarus was his favorite and he would read it over and over.

"Why did he do that? Raise Lazarus who had been dead four days and had begun to smell?"

Myrna and I didn't know and Billy looked baffled enough and just twitched.

"Why, because he loved him!" When it came to quizzing us on the reading, it seemed Leeland always asked and answered his own questions. "When Jesus came to Mary and Martha's and found his friend gone four days, he cried, suffered from human grief. And raised Lazarus because he wanted him alive. Not in the next world, but in this one, where he could be with him some more. And he wanted to tell us, too, to get our minds on life in the here and now. Not life in some place which for all we know may come with some of the same old problems. He was telling us that our concerns here were not with 'afterlife.' But just with life, that it's all of a piece for us to weave and with help, maybe into something good."

Standing in Kress's in my ninety something or another year, I remembered Leeland saying all that, heard it, though the rooming house where we had lived and the park next to it, was gone, was memory. Was a parking lot! Just concrete like so much else that used to be green or blue or multi-colored (at Eastertime all flowered all over). Some greedy thief would have paved over water for a dollar!

"Well," I said to Renato who was rearranging the scarves, and I don't know how long I had been standing in front of him as all this came back to me, "your relatives are not the only ones who have gone, looks to me like everything and everybody I ever knew in Corpus Christi has been blown away. Tell me, though, do the city buses still run?"

Maybe the buses were memory, too! If they weren't, I wanted, after I got settled, to take one up the hill, behind the stores on Chaparral Street and inland down Leopard to Palm Drive, never the best side of town and probably gone down further, which even in my

15

time had precious few palms on it — and I had heard more had died of blight — where the Bells and all of us used to live. Palm had boasted some pretty yards for a neighborhood of working people and the Bells always had the prettiest because of Leeland's baby brother, Bo's love of gardening. And it was with Bo with whom Mother and Daddy Bell and I and Bo's niece, Elizabeth (his sister's child), came to live.

"The buses run every twenty minutes," Renato said, "and every which way."

"Do they still go out Leopard?"

He nodded that they did.

I was glad of that. I didn't have enough money with me to spend much on taxis which I told Renato. But since I didn't feel up to walking much more, I thought I might take one this evening and I also asked him if I could get a taxi over to my motel on Shoreline Drive.

Renato told me that city buses only came as far as Chaparral and the Kress's store, that it was the end of the line. But he said I didn't need one. He said that after I had my sundae, he would walk me to the corner where I could get a trolley. He would be off soon, he told me, and trolleys which only cost a nickel ran from Chapparal up and down Shoreline all day.

"That's good, honey," I told him. "Tomorrow I want to go over on the seawall and find a good empty spot to do some fishing. And if you sell them, before I leave Kress's, I'll pick out a rod and reel. I need a real good fishing pole."

I thought maybe it was to catch a big fish that Leeland told me to come to Corpus Christi for.

From the End of the Line

Or was it to meet Renato, who got off work right after I had my sundae and walked me to a tackle store where we picked out my rod and reel? (A red one, honey.) Held me under the arm and guided me like a grandson.

The truth is, from our first conversation I felt as if I had known him all my life, as if he was in the Kress's store waiting for us to pick up from where we had left off in some long ago time. When I first met Leeland I felt like that, too.

One thing I knew the boy understood: fishing lines, told me right away he didn't think Kress's had anything I could use, walked me up the street to a tackle store — he didn't seem to mind going slow — and tested three different rods before he found one on sale he thought would do for the thirty dollars I had to spend and after I paid the storekeeper, saw me to the trolley which rolled right down Shoreline just like he said it would and I waved good-bye to him as it pulled away.

"I'll come to see you," I told him. "Maybe I'll have something good to tell." Though the town I remembered was gone, the new Shoreline just a place for those passing through, Renato and I connected. I felt close to the boy all of a sudden, glad to have him in Corpus Christi. In my life story he had become an important person. I was more than at the age to consider my life story, the mystery of it, had been considering it for some time, but had none to think about it on the trolley as I had to get off just a little while after I got on. Inside the Ramada I found dust in the corners and the molding peeling. Considering what Searcy was paying, the place should have been better kept. I called him right away to say everything was all right, and then ate a simple scrambled egg supper in the plainest of dining rooms. Not a flower on a table or a vegetable on the menu. Just meat and potatoes and South Texas drab brown. I considered looking for some paper flowers the next time I was in Kress's to fix it up.

After supper I sat in the hot, sticky air by the swimming pool, my back to the bay front and the tourists on their trolleys, my back to the wind. And the trellis behind me protected me from it. This was

July, darlin', one of the last before my heart just quit (back in East Texas on a January 1).

I just sat staring at the block in front of the one I was on and at what used to be the old Nueces and what was now the Nueva Nueces, the hotel still as pink as that scarf I bought, but part of it also aquamarine, and at the block in front of that, the top of Kress's, the letters K R E S S across the front in red, a couple of gulls swooping down toward them from the big gray clouds that covered the sky.

The sky had been gray and clouded all through this day when I had been traveling and the streets here were gray and the water when I turned my head to view it, and except for a couple which were brown, all the tall buildings. And my spirits more or less. Renato and his scarves and the bright cotton leaves and the flowers of the field had been the day's only colors. Renato had part of my name; that struck me as strange as I sat thinking of him. Already he had entered the past.

I shut my eyes then so I could also enter and be in the town as I used to know it when I lived with the Bells at mid-century.

Once or twice a week in the 1950s I rode a city bus to the end of its line, then transferred and began all over. And for a few hours got away from those people in that family which through Leeland, though he was gone from us all, had become mine. I had always liked riding buses, used to ride them when I was a child in southern Louisiana near Vermilion Bay to get away from my mother who we called Mammy and my brother, Johnny, and my little sister, Lucy. And we were all close. But, you know, to live with family, even those in it you care for most, can be to live with tyranny. Time came when I just had to be by myself and free.

"Rena, where do you go when you ride the bus?" Leeland's mother always asked me.

"Why, to the picture show," I told her, "or sometimes just downtown to walk through Kress's." In those days I bought myself a new picture puzzle to work on (how I learned patience, darlin') or a new shade of rouge. Or I talked to the birds in their cages.

Ellen Bell, you know, once loved a canary; sometimes I thought that bird was all besides her sewing she had any feeling for. She talked sweet to him sometimes, the way she never talked to people.

18

But a yard cat got him one day when she put his cage on the front porch for sun. And she just said to Elizabeth, "Go find me a cigar box, and then go outside and in the back of the flower bed, dig a deep hole." The loss must have hurt her, though she never let on. Oh, she seemed a block of wood, darlin'.

But I often asked myself how she got that way. Was it from, as a child maybe, an excess of grief? Seems like people who feel too much, and get a bad hurt early, forever after can't feel at all.

Sometimes I looked at the canaries in Kress's thinking I would get Ellen Bell one. But finally decided against it and spent what money I had on cosmetics and puzzles and berries with frozen cream.

And whether I was at the lunch counter at Kress's or at a show or just on a bus looking out at houses and yards or seawall and water, I always met somebody who liked to laugh and have a good time, somebody I could enjoy. Speaking to people always came naturally to me, and I liked being spoken to.

"Mother Bell," I used to say to Ellen Bell, for that's what everyone called her, "whenever I go out on an excursion I almost always meet somebody." Oh, her lip curled up at that! "Well, now, what's wrong?" I asked her. "What's the matter with a little conversation?"

One of my favorite rides was to Six Points — buses from there shot out in six directions — where I transferred to a bus that went out Ocean Drive all the way to the Naval Air Station. I enjoyed good conversation for the better part of the day, and as often as not, wound up with someone for supper. Oh, I talked with all kinds, men and women, teen-agers and old folk, Mexicans and plain white people and sometimes, when I sat near the back of the bus, some colored. You know, Mammy was part black, had been born in Cajun country where some slaves had first gone free and where black and white spoke French to each other and went to Mass together. Mammy spoke some French and a little Spanish, but seldom to us children, so not much from those languages passed to me.

But I always loved riding the buses with all the people! Lord, you have to get out of your own skin once in a while, break free from your own kind, your own family, before it turns you against everything and everybody who is different from you.

Elizabeth agreed, but thought sometimes I went too far. Sometimes she warned me. Said, "Aunt Rena, you have to be careful, have to be a little careful sometimes of strangers." (This was forty years ago, what would she say about the world today?) Then she reminded me of the stranger I married right after Leeland died, that man I met at the track who took me for a rich widow. God knows that insurance money I put on the horse was all Leeland left me, all I had. (And right after Leeland died, I felt so bad I spent some of it on a trip to Acapulco.)

Before Jack Dubuffet took me to the bank, he took me to the nightclubs — and was a beautiful dancer. But I should have quit him on the dance floor. Leeland drank too much when he got discouraged and said things that hurt sometimes — and what I said back and his drinking sometimes took him to other women. But he never hit me, darlin'.

"You don't need to worry," I told Elizabeth, "I'm never going out with the likes of that man again. Don't trouble your head over your Aunt Rena."

Elizabeth worried more than any of them in that workhouse and in that family that I stayed in even after Leeland died because I loved him and because, through him, it had become mine. She was an only child, an only grandchild and they counted on her too much. I saw her life slipping away.

I would say to her, "Honey, life can't be all work and no play. And there's no proof at all it's serious. Now your school this week is over, so why don't you go on down to the waterfront with a friend?"

And she would say, shaking her black hair already shot through with gray and she was just fifteen, darlin', "Oh, Aunt Rena, I can't go by myself. Some boy has to take me. I know that's dumb, but that's the way it is."

"Well," I would tell her, "it's Friday afternoon and the buses are running and your Aunt Rena is going for a ride."

Some Fridays I took the bus up Leopard and met Bill Powers, a friend of mine, who ate in the cafeteria on the hill, just behind the Driscol Hotel where the movie star with a similar last name stayed.

When I first came back to Corpus to live with the Bells, and this was after Leeland died and after I was in and out of legal ties with that no good Dubuffet, I got off the bus there at the cafeteria because I wanted a good vegetable dinner. I had always loved vegetables. (When I was just a little girl I tended our vegetable garden, and before I was in my teens planted one of my own.) And that cafeteria had every kind: okra, fried or with tomatoes, turnips in a sweet white sauce, and white onion rings in vinegar, kale with bacon, and Texas slaw, and every kind of green.

One evening when I was there after I returned to Corpus, I started a conversation with the fellow at the table next to me. I had noticed him there before and observed that all he ever ate was pie, coconut cream and blackberry cobbler (how I once loved to pick berries to make that. Met Leeland in a blackberry thicket.) And pecan. And chocolate banana. Ever hear of that? Two or three kinds on the same tray! Oh, maybe he would also have a chicken leg sometimes or mashed potatoes. But never anything green. Or yellow. Or any healthy color.

"Honey," I said as I passed him, just before I sat down at a neighboring table with my tray, "honey, you are going to get sick this way."

"Well," he said, sticking his fork in a piece of chocolate pie and pushing it toward me, "I sure don't want to do that, so why don't you eat a piece of this for me?"

I sat next to him because he looked so lonely. Something about his expression reminded me of Leeland. Leeland, near the end, after he had stopped drinking, all but lived on pie. And Bill was lanky like Leeland, too, who no matter how much pie he ate, never gained any weight. Also like Leeland, he was with women at first a little bit shy. I could tell by the way he turned color when he spoke.

"Maybe I will," I said, "I've forgotten my dessert. I'll exchange these mustard greens for it." When he shook his head I said, "Eat them, now, they're good for you." And so he tried them. And began to talk, in between bites and making ugly faces.

Before I knew it, he had in his shy way, told me some of his life story. Like Leeland, he was also a veteran of the first war. His giving up the bottle and craving sweets after was like Leeland, too. His wife died of a sunstroke the year before when she made an August visit to her sister in Dallas; she just keeled over on a city sidewalk one hundred degree Saturday afternoon when they had gone shopping and she never came to. Their only child, a naval air pilot, was shot down in the South Pacific, Corregidor, in War II. I told Bill then that I was a person who understood about the terrible loss of children. I told him about Juliette, my baby who died all those years ago and about Searcy's little boy who I took care of years later, being run over by a bus. And I told him about meeting Leeland years after Juliette died and about my life with him and about the man I met and married, though it was no real marriage, after. I thought I made it, I told him, as an escape from grief. After it was over I escaped some more by running off to Mexico as I had years ago after my baby died, and I told him about that, too. And about coming back to live with the Bells after.

By the time I was through telling, all the pie had disappeared. "Do you like to play cards?" I asked him. "I have a deck in my pocket." I had bought it just the week before at Kress's. "We could have a game or two at one of the tables down in the park next to the picture show."

He had come to the cafeteria on foot because he lived in an old house on Tancuhua or Carancahua, I forget which — two streets in Corpus have those Indian names — and when I slept in that house as I did later I heard the Indians singing in the trees, songs of young Indians, real Corpus natives, who seemed to have risen from the very ground.

Next thing I knew we were walking down the bluff toward the Ritz and by dusk playing pitch — the game Leeland and Daddy and I most liked to play — at the table nearest the rooming house where Leeland and I once lived and we talked about meeting there the next afternoon for a show. Matinees were cheap and air-conditioned, a good way to beat the heat and pass the time.

"We could play horseshoes here after," I suggested, "or take a bus to Shoreline and play miniature golf."

After that I saw him now and then, but not every Saturday. And months passed after I first talked to him until the time I went to his old Tancuhua house. I think it was Tancuhua and not Carancahua that the house was on. I don't recall which, but I do remember it was a pretty place, built in the early part of the century with these great big rooms and twelve-foot ceilings and at night young Indian spirits whispering and singing and telling stories out in the biggest live oak trees. Oh, it's gone now, trees and all. The freeway's come right through the place where it was standing whichever street it was on. So the spirits had to move on. But I wondered where to. Where did spirits go when they lost their quiet places along with their trees and ground?

Through my life I asked that question many times and had no answer. Anyway, before that place where those spirits liked to talk and sing (where I could hear them, darlin') was paved over with concrete, my friend, Bill Powers, one sticky summer evening gave a neighborhood party, threw a barbecue in his backyard and opened his house, all those big, old downstairs rooms, for dancing. I made a fruit salad and a slaw, but he tended to all the rest, meat and toast and pinto beans.

At first just youngsters took to the dancing — Bill Powers had cleared the great big dining room for it — then some of us older ones joined them. I enjoyed the party so much I stayed on for a long time after supper, went on dancing with Bill before I helped him clean up the kitchen, then remembered that was how I got started with that no good Dubuffet.

Then when Bill Powers first ran a hand down my back as I was washing the dishes, I turned against him and said, "You sure do feel good, darlin', but I want you to know I don't get in situations like this often." Before I even came to his house I let him know that although I had been legally tied to three partners, two bad men I didn't really care about, one when I was too young and the other when I was too old to know any better, and one good one I loved, as far as I was concerned, I had only been married one time. And one time was all I wanted. "I haven't had casual relations with many," I told him. I knew the Bells thought differently. "And never mind my age."

Then he leaned real near — all this, you understand, was at the kitchen sink full of dirty dishes. "God knows I can't compete with the sainted dead," he whispered (he didn't know how soon he was going to join them), "with that man you'll always be married to, so maybe it's time to start."

Fishing

Photo by Susan Bright

From the Seawall: One

How jealous would that have made Leeland? That's the question I asked that morning at the seawall after I first threw in my line. Asked the wind how jealous did it make him?

Bill Powers was a nice man to be with, but he wasn't Leeland, who I couldn't be near, let alone touch, who was gone, darlin'. I reasoned that since Leeland was in a country without flesh, or at least that's the way I understood it then, whatever I did with Bill Powers while I was still in mine, might be ok.

My body gave me pleasure, but also pleasure's opposite — doesn't everybody's? And on lots of days, I thought I would be just as glad to leave it. But not during that long summer when the heat in Corpus, to say nothing of between Bill Powers and me, stretched into October which was the month he died. Maybe joined his wife or some other person in that other region.

I found him slumped over the kitchen table one hundred degree Friday when I dropped by for a cold supper: boiled shrimp on beds of lettuce over ice, that's what he said when he called, and when I got to his house, that's what I found in the refrigerator. "We'll go to a show," he had told me, "if you know a good one that is playing, maybe an old mystery."

Instead, after calling the coroner, I spent the evening at the funeral home across from the park. And when Billy Park saw me, he came leaping across the street making back of the throat noises, trying so hard to cry out when he saw Bill Powers stretched out on a slab inside. (Honey, because of the heat, when the coroner found Bill had an insurance policy and I knew just where that was, he got him straight to the funeral parlor so they could go to work on him right away.)

"Don't cry, Billy," I said and put an arm around the poor boy's shoulders because he was wailing so hard.

He pointed to Bill Powers' chest and toward mine, touched the breast above my heart. Awful sounds came out of his mouth, came from way in the back of it. "You" and "Friend" or "Your Friend." Those were the words I think he was trying to say.

"Billy, honey," I said, "he was your friend. He was just plain friendly." And lonesome, I thought, as I sometimes was, and I knew Billy, too. "We'll miss him." I wanted to add that he got through death fast and expecting something pleasant. A cold shrimp dinner and a cheerful mystery in the air-conditioned picture show.

Because I had so much to do comforting Billy, I pushed my own feelings about the loss of Bill Powers down. "If it feels good," I told Billy, contradicting what I had said earlier, "just bawl."

The funeral director, when he heard Billy, had little patience and made signs to me to take him out. Since I couldn't answer many of the questions he asked about Bill's relatives, anyway — I only knew about his dead son and wife — I saw Billy across the street quick as I could and into Myrna's where Myrna and I drank a little beer and Billy kept crying and crying while guzzlin' *7-Up*. Myrna wept some, too. I didn't. I expect I was still in shock, but somehow I was also happy for Bill, that he had accomplished what most dread so easily and with so little fuss.

Myrna, Billy and I were the only ones at the private service at the funeral home on Sunday morning. (I arranged it, darlin'.) In connection with Bill's death I got my name in the Saturday paper which reported that "a friend, Rena Bell Dubuffet," found the corpse. (You can imagine what the Bells said about that.) The movie Bill and I missed was "Charlie Chan in Rio," which I had seen anyway five or six years before, part of a Charlie Chan festival the Ritz was putting on that October and a re-release.

Rena Bell Dubuffet. As I sat by the seawall I used to say my name out loud like that. But while the name rang out, even with the wind blowing, I stayed curled up inside myself separate from it.

But ready to break out. Ready to break through, darlin'.

Used to say my name. And Leeland's. And my runaway brother, Johnny's, who long ago disappeared into Mexico. Half believed if I said it often enough I'd summon him near. And the names, Searcy and Johnny Two (after his lost uncle), children of my little sister, Lucy — I called her "Clarity" because her name meant light (I found this out from a naming book Mammy was always reading) — who slipped away from us into water, whose sweet face I saw rising that morning over Corpus Christi Bay.

When we were children we set up an altar to the Sun Queen in our front yard where it was most of the year so hot and bright that we were sure a queen from the sun ruled over it. We pulled one of the yard benches to the center of our grass front and set fruit jars filled with water from the porch spigot on it and stuck oleander or canna or sunflowers, or just whatever, besides weeds, happened to be growing there.

And we knelt down before our altar and threw our heads back, and we looked up toward the sun and spread our hands in front of our faces, opening our fingers so that pieces of broken colored light spilled through them and over us. When Clarity, as I called her, slipped away from us and into Vermilion Bay as she did years later, I said the Sun Queen must have seen her do it and dipped down after to take her off.

And sure enough, her face rose before me there over the water. She always looked pretty, but this time, troubled, too. Was she just there to greet me? I wondered. Was there something she wanted to say?

In my mind I called to her. And said: Lucy, I've missed you. But I've enjoyed your children. Looked after them after you drowned.

They were sweet boys and became good men, caring and steady. We lost your only grandchild, Searcy's son. Your Johnny couldn't have children and never did adopt any; his business and his wife, Maurine, became his life. I didn't know if our brother, Johnny, ever had any.

I went searching for him in Mexico after my baby, Juliette, died and I broke away from my first husband. And I went looking for Johnny again a long time later, after your Johnny Two and Searcy were grown up and Leeland was dead and I had married and then left Jack Dubuffet whose name I still carry.

Somehow I didn't think to look on my trip to Acapulco right after Leeland's passing — I was crazed with grief. But all the times I traveled there, I found a lot in that country and across it. Monterrey to Veracruz to Jalisco. A lot that stirred my heart, and clarified my thinking the way you used to do when we were little. Remember how you did that for me?

Remember the day I learned I failed Algebra, and almost failed Latin, brought home an F and a D on my report card, and lay down on one side of my own little garden, the one I had planted and started digging, trying to plant myself maybe, trying to make more of me, digging and thrashing, making myself a pit in the ground, digging myself into a hole?

(Never mind that you were younger. You explained things so that they would come clear when I was all mixed up and had thrown some fit.)

That day I felt such a failure in my own garden — lettuce and tomato plants on the other side of me, and all kinds of flowers. (I had just scattered some mixed seeds in between the vegetable rows.) I might have dug a grave for myself, sure enough, if I hadn't heard your voice, felt your hand on one shoulder.

"Ree-nee, Ree-nee," (what you always called me), "look around you. What do you care about some old school subjects?"

I raised my head to better catch the sound, and when I did I saw through the dirt a stream of light and the colors breaking in it that seemed to come from you, and the vegetables that had given us such good big salads (and fresh buttered carrots and the best red tomatoes for chicken stew) and the sprightly flowers. (I had never done a thing but water and pull a few weeds.) And I crawled out of the earth instead of going farther in it. I'd let the dirt fall in on me; dirt was what I thought I wanted instead of air.

Mexico in some way said to me: who you are is ok (even a help) — the way you did, Lucy, when we were growing up.

But I never did find our brother. And he never presents himself. Nor none of the rest. Since you had special powers here, I expect you also have them where you are now, and that's why I can see you.

That was a lot to tell the wind and Lucy, even if I didn't do the telling out loud, but only sent a message with my mind. And on my very first day back in Corpus Christi!

But her face, darlin', and her presence was on that morning, just as it had been when we grew up together, so clear. Made me want to put down my rod and reel and reach out to touch it. And would have if it had been a little closer instead of way out over some waves.

When I lived with the Bells in the 1950s and took the bus down to the seawall, Lucy's face sometimes rose like that, too. And though I was glad to see her, I was never startled.

In those days the buses ran the whole way, so when I didn't stop to see Myrna Teague who stayed on in the rooming house where I had lived with Leeland or to visit Billy Park, I would come right on down to the seawall.

As I guess I've told you, Billy's mind was bent a little, like one of his legs, and he didn't hear or speak much — read lips to understand. But he leaped around the park like a forest creature on the leg that was good and on a cane. And he kept the park clean. Sometimes Myrna and I helped him do it and had a good time, Billy, a real cut-up who, except for that day when he walked in on the corpse of Bill Powers, always seemed happy. He told jokes in signs.

Bill Powers especially liked to have fun with Billy; he'd hop around the picnic tables with him, picking up plastic forks and an occasional beer can that didn't make the garbage, or paper plates — shaking his fist at the imagined litter bug responsible, sometimes even pretending to be a police officer. Watching him and Billy play-act was good entertainment and cheaper than the picture show. Billy always skipped ahead right on out to the sidewalk in front of the Ritz if he saw Bill Powers and me coming and it was Bill he hugged — no wonder Billy cried so when he saw he couldn't do that anymore! He was too shy to hug me, though I always got a big smile.

In the years gone before, Billy was shy around Leeland, who always shook his hand when he saw him in the park; Billy never touched Leeland that I remember except to take his extended hand in the good, strong handshake Leeland was known for, and often looked down when Leeland spoke. But they say Billy went on his first, and as far as anyone knows, his only bender when he heard that Leeland died. This was what Myrna told me when I came back to town. Billy, as I remember him, was a teetotaler.

On nights when Myrna and Billy Park weren't around or when I just wanted to be solitary — and as much as I took to people, there were lots of times like that — I would come here, to the seawall, to talk to the wind and for some fishing. Unless the fish were nice and small, the size I could pan fry for Myrna or Billy — the Bells didn't like fish much (Ellen Bell couldn't stand the smell) — I always threw back whatever tugged on my line. What I liked was not so much the fishing — to tell the truth, it always hurt me to see anything die, even the flounder which was so delicious. What I liked was talking, talking in my head or right out loud, that and just looking into the water and the sky.

Sitting on the seawall with a good line like the one Renato had picked out for me, that's when I brought up memory after I cast deep down.

From the Seawall: Two

Rena Bell Dubuffet, who are you?

Seemed almost as if that was the question the wind was always asking.

And only I was there to answer. Well, as far as children are concerned, an aunt seemed to be the role I was meant to play. My baby girl, Juliette, tore me all up when she was born, and afterwards I developed an infection, so that before I was twenty I had to have a hysterectomy.

Juliette's father called me a "dumb Creole" and sometimes a "dumb nigger," and had no respect for me or for much of anything living. Why did I, Rena Brock, who was brought up in an ordinary family, a mostly loving family, marry a man like that? And why did Mammy let me? By the time I did it, our big brother, Johnny, was in Texas and Papa J — that's what we called our daddy — was gone.

Because we were ignorant, darling. Because we didn't know.

In those days everyone thought a young girl should marry, should be "protected." If she did, everyone called her "safe." And when the man first asked Mammy for me, she thought he would be a good husband. He came from people who were well known in our parish and he had a little money.

Mammy was, I know now, flattered that he had asked, and believed he could give me more than what I had. Our farm had never done much more than feed us if the weather was right. And with Johnny and Papa J gone, it was hard for us to care for more than a few chickens and a garden. Mammy thought I should have a man who was a little older. He was thirty-two and so good looking. Green eyes and black hair. I didn't know much about what men and women did together — and he was sure no one to teach me — but I liked his looks, had a yen for him, so I thought marriage would be fine.

But he wasn't tender, darlin'. The man wasn't tender. From the beginning that's the way I thought of it, that I had left a tender family to cast my lot with some other kind. What sort, I asked then (and still do), was it?

I never found out completely. All I know is that after our

wedding, a small candlelight service in the Catholic church, instead of driving to New Orleans like he promised, he stopped at a cheap hotel in the next town and before I had even taken off my traveling clothes just held me down on the bed. And hurt me, darlin'. Body and heart. Why did he want me? It took me some time to learn why, but I finally did. Because my blood was mixed. What did he want me for? To have someone to hurt and not get arrested for it. And to have someone to treat like a whore.

This took me a while to realize because he had put on such a show with Mammy and me before we married and went to N.O. to live. (Yes, in the Quarter, darlin'; he played cards for money there.) But when I was pretty sure I was pregnant, a dark-skinned girl who looked like Lucy came to me in a dream and told me to watch out. And not long after, that man took off with another woman, someone he met in the Quarter (and to tell you the truth I was glad of it) and when he came back to our rooms to get his things, he hit me across the face when I said I wanted to leave, too. After he struck me, he held me down on the bed, like he had the first night we were married and rammed me hard and after he was finished (and I lay curled up in a ball, hurt and sobbing), he slapped some bills down on the bedside table and called me "nigger" and some other bad names, darlin'. (I don't want to repeat them here.) And then said I was legally his to do with as he liked and that he expected me to stay there and wait for him to maybe come back when he had a mind to. Someone would be in to check on me, he said.

"You are just a woman," he told me, "and inferior." (Yes, he said that, darlin'.) "When my friend comes round to see about you, I want you to open the door," — he locked it when he stepped out — "and do for him whatever he asks."

Well, there was no way I was going to let myself in for his friend, darlin'. I took the money he left and after throwing a valise that held most of my clothes out of a window, lifted myself through it and then slid down the drain pipe at the side of the building and went to live up the country with our cousins, all dark brown or blue black — they had that much more black blood than Mammy. I hadn't visited them since I was a child, but that dream gave me directions, and the route it marked out took me right there.

I didn't tell them, or anybody about the baby. Didn't tell a living soul. But, of course, Juliette finally showed and I could feel her and began to love her even though she was his — after all, she couldn't help who she was related to and I reasoned even he wasn't born perverted and mean. (I found out he grew up with cruelty, darlin'.) I began to think I should go back to Mammy and Lucy who I thought I needed for the baby to be OK. But though I longed for them, I didn't go.

My cousins didn't taunt me about my condition — I never told them I was married, I was ashamed to have married — and I was grateful they took me in without asking questions and that they let me alone.

But they didn't know a doctor to get me to after I fell from running when I thought I saw that man coming after me. Saw his shadow everywhere. (Seems from the time I was very young I was always seeing shadows.) I imagined that, darlin', afraid as I was all the time. Yet out of panic I ran on.

Ran and ran. But finally tripped over a tree limb fallen in the road and had to turn around and drag myself home. And Juliette came early and just tore me apart. (The midwife didn't know the right things to do, and I got an infection and later on, after I got back to Mammy but was still having trouble, had my uterus out.)

Juliette was a pretty child, but sickly. Colicky and prone to rashes and the croup. Then she contracted scarlet fever. And after awhile she died. I didn't go home right away to Mammy and Lucy — I was too ashamed — and they didn't know how to find me. For a time with the last of the money that man left me, the hundreds he had slapped down on the table by our bed, I ran off to Mexico, a crazy girl who didn't know where she was going, or what she would run into. And I'll tell you about that sometime, honey.

Leeland married me knowing I could never again have a child, and he said, not caring. After a long time together we were given his sister's child, Elizabeth, to care for. At least for awhile. Elizabeth lost her daddy, and for a time, her mother who during the Depression years went to work in South Texas (the only place where there was any) while Mother and Daddy Bell and Leeland and I stayed in Hot Springs.

Elizabeth and I seemed destined for one another.

Before I met Leeland, awhile after I lost the baby, I did go home where I told Mammy and Lucy, too, my troubles. They were glad to see me, darlin', had all but given up on me. That man I married had been to see them, told them some awful story about me and that I had run off. Mammy hadn't thought about me being with her cousins who we hadn't seen since I was a little child. I don't know how I remembered them, darlin'. Only through the dream, I guess.

By this time Lucy had married and had two little boys just a year apart, Searcy and Johnny, the second, who I called Johnny Two. (Maybe he should have been Johnny Three since our father's name was John.) But her husband who she met because she was a healer — he was tubercular, honey — crashed his pick-up into an oak when he slid off the road. He had been in the woods to pick up a Christmas tree and everybody thought he had been drinking a little. Some people in our family went all of a sudden. Something to do with the stream of energy we got born in — falling off places in it — that's what Mammy believed and told me.

A few years later when Lucy couldn't heal herself of typhoid fever — oh, people died young of awful diseases! — it affected her brain so that she took to getting up from her sick bed and wandering away and once to swimming. I reasoned she wandered to the river because she was burning hot and was caught in a whirly place and just went down in the water.

And now rises over it. Has maybe been rising over it somewhere ever since. Brown-skinned like Mammy and light-eyed like our papa. A shine on her face even after dark.

Oh, who was she, darlin'? Besides my sister and Searcy's Mama, and Johnny Two's. Who was she and where is she now? And where is our brother, Johnny? He seemed my other half, me almost, but a different side.

I see you before me, Johnny, hear you calling, "Come on." See you darting through the trees, Lucy and me after you, jars in our hands to capture fireflies.

I always saw you before me whenever I struck out, took a chance.

Searcy stared and stared at that face in the pictures we had kept of Lucy. Of her two boys, he took the loss of her hardest. Asked me to tell him all I could remember about her. And I told him how she had prevented me from burying myself in our flower and vegetable garden — he laughed when he heard how I had tried to do that — and how when she was just a baby she straightened an old man's legs just by wrapping herself around them. Some say he had been depressed and needed someone, anyone, even a baby, to take an interest in him. But never mind how she did it, after she wrapped herself around that old man's legs and crawled up onto his lap, giggling, he ever afterward walked straight. And came to visit her with candy and presents every day.

I went through all the pictures I had kept of Lucy in an old shoe box and found one of her with this man holding her, him standing up on his legs straight as you please. And then I showed him a head shot of Lucy and in color when she was pink cheeked and radiant, taken just before he was born.

And later when I began to see her in the world — as I did that morning in Corpus Christi — I told Searcy, sometimes, about it.

All of us are different in our needs. Honey, from the beginning this boy needed me, needed to hear about my visions, needed my storytelling in a way that his brother, Johnny Two, did not.

From the Seawall: Three

Beautiful. Lucy's face was, like always. But this time I thought I also saw some trouble in it. Her lips moved, but no sound came from them. I needed Billy Park with me to know what she was trying to say.

Back in "Bell Family Time," the 50s, I also saw Lucy rising over the waves of Corpus Christi Bay, also saw her dark skin shining and her mess of auburn hair. She looked just the same back then — except for the worried expression — arms open, beckoning, lips parted. (But her lips didn't move, only looked as if they were about to.) Which raised this question. Is an instant of eternal time like fifty years in time I then knew? Maybe so, though I still don't have a sure answer, darlin'.

Both times she rose while all that teeming stuff teemed on underwater. If you dive far down, like I used to when I was a girl in Louisiana, you see that life for the creatures of the deep is violent and terrible and that they spend their whole time chasing after and away from another, killing and consuming as they can (though way far down are places where they sometimes sleep), just living out a horror story. Even back in "Bell Family Time," I saw Lucy rising over that.

Back then I asked Elizabeth who was just a teenager, "What did she want of me? What was she about to say?"

And Elizabeth answered, "She was about to say, 'Rena, take me out of this hateful bay where every creature feeds on every other and I have to dart between fish hooks besides!'" (Oh, darlin', to think my hook was one of them.) Later Elizabeth told me that if there turned out to be such a thing as reincarnation — and this in spite of all the Christians in the world who said there wasn't — she hoped she would be spared a new life, however short, as a creature of the sea. Then as an after thought, added, she supposed jungles and woods weren't much safer.

"No," I told her, "and in some places, or so I've heard, not even city streets." I was thinking of parts of New Orleans and what I had heard about Chicago and New York City. (And of the whole world, or at least a whole lot of it, during World War II.)

Sometimes when Elizabeth involved me in these conversations I considered the fish-terror at the heart of life a force that we're all driven by. But, honey, it'll drive you crazy if you think about that too much, and most of the time when Elizabeth got on that subject, I tried to change it.

Up in Arkansas where Leeland and I lived for a long time after we first married, Elizabeth was like my very own child. Even when she was little more than a baby, she toddled from Ellen Bell's house to mine, which sat next to Ellen's, came right up to my front door. I tended her most of the time when she was little before she went down to South Texas to live with her mama who was teaching music in the schools. Knew all the time that finally I would hand her over to her mama and to others, but that's what all caretakers of children do or ought to whether they are the natural parents or relatives of the natural parents or not.

Elizabeth was a teen-ager by the time I came back to the Bells and when she asked why I liked to take off so much on buses, I said, "Honey, I just have to get out of this place where they all stay too much with each other, and you should get out, too." I told her I always urged my nephews, Lucy's boys, Searcy and Johnny, to get out in the world and make friends, although of course I didn't want them running so far off I could never be with them — like Johnny had — didn't want them running all the way out of this country and through Mexico.

Unless, of course, they were called to go.

Johnny Two and Searcy I took care of before I married Leeland, and they were good children who grew up to be good, steady men. But to tell you the truth, I always thought they were a little too somber. Johnny Two, especially, who made such a success in business, maybe because he didn't want to be a runaway Texas wildcatter or crazed silver miner or just a no good drunken drifter like many said the uncle he was named after was. (I never believed those people, honey.) Searcy liked doing ordinary jobs, was more like me that way.

I was happy working in a department store as an alteration lady, taking up hems that were too long, or taking out seams on pants that were too tight. And I never minded the job I had as a receptionist with the telephone company in Shreveport, could talk to a lot of different people in the course of a day — though that's where I was the morning Searcy's little boy was killed, run over by a city bus because the woman I paid to look after him wasn't. I felt responsible all the same.

Is there something in me, I asked, that works to kill children? First Juliette. And then little Newt, Searcy's son.

I had come back to Louisiana to be with Searcy and his boy when Leeland was on a job way up north somewhere — I believe some place near Chicago. I was put out with him because of his hard drinking and what I thought he might be doing with the women he met when he left Elizabeth at Sunday school and disappeared into a nearby drinking club (a place where he could bring his own bottle). I had never liked cold weather, and I believed a short separation — maybe just through the winter — might do us good.

Searcy thought I could help him and little Newt out, but I knew in order for us all to make it, I had to work part time. Little Newt's mama died when he was born. She had him at home without good help, the way a lot of women did, and she got a fever and it went too high.

But I'm leaping ahead in time. Maybe you'll get used to me leaping ahead like Billy Park and then hopping backward like Billy did sometimes, too. Whatever happened to Billy? I wonder if he lived on much longer. I can still see him leaping for Bill Powers when he saw him, right into his arms!

All this I now tell you was years after I lost Juliette, my own baby. I lived a long time, nearly eleven years, without a steady man before I met Leeland.

I hadn't known Leeland a week when I knew clear through me that he was it, my natural connection, and though I didn't know why and never found out, he did turn out to be. Just who was he? (Besides Mother and Daddy Bell's son, I mean.) That remains mysterious, darlin', as you will see.

When we lived together in Arkansas and Texas, we were poor and he dreamed too much — I never knew why, or what that ambition was that fired through and tormented him — drew up too many plans for buildings no one commissioned or even wanted.

40

Once after a week of hard drinking — and, honey, he could put away a fifth of whiskey in an afternoon — he went into that place he called his "office," just a narrow hallway where we kept the ice box and where the iceman came twice a week to drop a big block in — that ran off the kitchen of our two-room pine board house (the one Leeland put up as a place to camp till we could do better after the bigger house we had burned down) and drew up plans for buildings in an underground city. He said the top of the world wouldn't be a fit place for people and that they would have to live in holes without natural air or light. (Sometimes when I looked around in some neighborhoods in the new Corpus Christi, I thought he might have been right and not just drunk or hungover.)

Drunk or sober, Leeland was always good to my family and glad to see Johnny, Jr. and Searcy when they came visiting and before she died, he put Mammy up for whole winters and summers at a time.

When I was growing up with her and my daddy, we were just an ordinary family. Our daddy, Papa J as we called him, had a small farm that fed us, but that's about all it did, we saw little profit from it, darlin'. And Mammy was happy just to do cooking and to make our clothes and to teach Lucy and me what she knew. She took a nap every afternoon after we had our dinner, which she had colored help in fixing, the big meal always being near the middle of the day when it was hot and not good for much but eating or sleeping. Papa J and our brother, Johnny — as I may have told you, Papa J's first name was Johnny, too — if he wasn't in school, who had come in from the field for dinner would sleep a little while after, too.

When Mammy got up, she sat on the porch and rocked and talked to us children or the neighbors, and sometimes as she spoke, she sewed scraps of material together. (Prepared me for the work I did later for those alteration places.) Following Mammy's lead, I got into the habit of talking then, of telling all I knew. And I learned piece work on that porch, pieced material, learning to work a needle and thread, and sometimes if I was tired of sewing, or there wasn't any, pieced together one of Mammy's jigsaw puzzles. (She bought one after another.) And, honey, I learned to put the pieces of lives together, too.

After the sun went down and Papa J came in, Johnny with him in the summertime when he wasn't in school, we made our supper mostly from leftovers in the cooler, and then we sometimes played a game of cards as Leeland and I came to do. Because it stayed light late, Johnny sometimes took me and Lucy to comb the woods in back of our house for wild greens and berries, and sometimes we trapped fireflies in jars. And Johnny liked to play hide and seek — always that streak of adventure in him! He'd run far from us.

Sometimes I thought it was only Mammy's calling that brought him back to us.

"Lucy! Rena! Johnny!" (Maybe that's when I learned to call out the names of those I missed, wanted to learn more about or wanted to see.) "Come in this house now."

It was getting dark. When Johnny heard our mother's voice, he would run straight to us.

"Come on. You heard. You want pie?"

If we came when she called, Mammy would serve us cobbler and milk before she heard prayers at bedtime. But if we lingered, we had to jump in bed and close our eyes at once, and take our chances on sleep without that comfort or, as far as we knew, blessing from either God or our mother.

But we didn't always have to get up early, never did on Sundays though someone had to gather eggs. (Us children took turns and sometimes fussed about who.) Papa J said he couldn't see getting up and then having nothing to do. During the week he worked the field early to miss the worst heat. He wasn't church going except for a few times a year and then he went to the Presbyterian where he had been raised. Mammy went to Mass every week, to the last one in the morning and often took at least one of us children, Johnny or me or Lucy, with her, though we never did study Catechism, not even when I went to Catholic school one year, and never were confirmed or made a First Communion in the Church. And we went on this way until just before I got married.

Then Johnny moved to get work. He was fed up with subsistence farming, he said, and wanted something good to do. Moved far from us, way down the Texas coast where he became an oil rigger and then a wildcatter, wrote letters to us from towns with names like Port Lavaca and Port Isabel. Finally, he drifted across the border (we heard from Matamoros; he said he would send money), then, I guess, all the way down into Mexico. We never heard after that.

But I couldn't believe he was gone from life like so many others.

(He was running drugs, honey, and I guess got himself into bad trouble, though I couldn't know that then.)

Papa J died and then my baby and then our darling Lucy. And many years later Searcy's wife died, too. Finally leaving just Searcy and me and for awhile, Mammy, to console each other, Johnny Two being all wrapped up in his wife, Maurine, and his farm machinery.

With our full lips and dark hair, Johnny and I looked something like our Mammy, but my round face, fair skin and blue eyes (blue-gray, darlin') I got from Papa J. Johnny was thin-faced and his eyes as brown and murky as the gravy on one of Papa J's stews. (Mammy taught me to make stew red from the tomatoes we grew and picked and put up in the summer, and to use fresh vegetables — green onion, bell pepper. I gave up eating red meat young, darlin', half a century before it came into fashion. Wrung the neck of many a chicken when I was a young woman — tried not to dwell on the killing I was doing — and kept a garden until the year before I died.)

Oh, people knew how to live when I was a girl in Louisiana. In Arkansas and Texas where I moved with Leeland, times grew hard, though before he began to drink so much, Leeland and I enjoyed being together and always had a good time, no matter how bad things were. I never really knew, honey, why he cared so much for me, just knew he did, was always astonished by that. I thought it too good to be true. Except when he was drinking, and what torment that came out of I never understood either, the time I spent with Leeland was prime.

But it always wore me out to be around his people. Ellen Bell ran a work house, sunup till sundown and suffered through the whole of every day, never seemed to enjoy a thing, not even listening to the radio or the Victrola in the evening when Leeland's daddy or Elizabeth liked to put records on. Just wore her grim face and talked about the neighbors, how she thought the people across the street drank beer in the evening and that the woman next door had strange looking callers.

"What do you care?" Elizabeth always asked. "What do you care who anybody sees or what they do?"

Well, she left the world like all the others and as everyone does. (All of us, honey.) All from the family are gone now except

Elizabeth who works a radio job somewhere in the west (western United States is what I'm referring to). Elizabeth is the last of the Bells — and I thought of her as a Bell, though her father wasn't. (He never figured in her life, darlin', he left before she was two.) When she was just a teenager I encouraged her to break away a little from them, to join herself to the human family. That, as things turned out, was what had always been in her to do. A good thing because she didn't marry.

In my oldest days when I moved to East Texas and lived near Searcy, I didn't hear from any of the Bells much, though Bo and Leona in their old age moved up to East Texas, too, and lived in a nearby town.

Of all the remaining family, at nearly a hundred I was the oldest. Leeland who died forty years before me had been Ellen's oldest child, the "Lee" in his name after General Lee — that's why they kept two "e"s in it — and never mind that Ellen Bell's own father fought in the Union army. Though some of the North was still in them and the West beckoned, Ellen and Daddy Bell named their first child after the Southland they had moved into.

Ellen Bell began in Southern Illinois, the youngest of twelve children and the only one who never had to work in the fields though she made clothes for the whole family. She married Leeland's Daddy who came to her county from southern Indiana with its Reb sympathies and took her down into southwestern Arkansas, and later to Texas. She said all her children were accidents: childbirth for her was never easy and the woman hated sex. She might have been abused when she was little by someone in her family. (That would explain a lot.) I never really knew.

But you would have thought that she would have at least welcomed her firstborn when he came into the world no matter what she had to go through to have him. Though she fed and clothed Leeland — and I guess in her own way loved him (loved him somehow in her head) — she kept herself distant from him. And I believe may have been relieved when he left home. Though Ellen Bell didn't like me, she never tried to lure Leeland from me, either. Leeland was his daddy's boy from the start. I was lucky that way, lucky I never had to put up with a mother-in-law who tried to snatch her son. Leeland looked to me for tenderness from a woman. (The women he met in those drinking places weren't real to him, darlin'.) Ellen Bell always said she would make Bo, her youngest child, born accidentally like the others but when she was facing menopause, a pleasure, train him to serve her, care for her in age. And oh, honey, did. And ruined his life. Bo, you know, never married. Outside the family never formed deep attachments.

I told myself that maybe all the Bells would relax a little when the time came for them to pass over. I hoped they would so as to have an easier time with the letting go they were going to have to do. And to maybe finally become more loving.

"Aunt Rena," Elizabeth asked me once, "are other races more loving?"

Well, what could I answer? We were meant for each other, Elizabeth and me, linked somehow (But I guess one way or another, all of us interconnect, darlin', more likeness between us than difference, no matter where we come from or what our blood.) People remarked on our physical resemblance, never realizing that my black hair was from my Creole mother and Elizabeth's from a black Scot daddy who, because he disappeared when she was a baby, she never knew.

Never realizing we were of different racial lines.

I knew Elizabeth had heard Ellen Bell talking about me saying I was part colored and then saying nasty things about the colored. But I also knew Elizabeth didn't put stock in what her grandmother said, that, in fact, if her grandmother told her something was so, she was likely to think the opposite true. Part of that was because her grandmother seldom showed her any sign of affection, or even much in the way of respect, though when she brought home her grades or evidence of some honor awarded to her, Ellen sometimes bestowed a smile or two.

So when Elizabeth asked if other races were more loving, what could I answer? I told her I thought loving might be more than we could ask most to do, but maybe we could ask that we treat each other decently. I said maybe if we did, the worst of the suffering would stop.

From the Seawall: Four

Just as I was thinking about this, I saw Renato coming to check on what I had caught. Only memory I would have to tell him, not another thing! Or maybe he was coming to check on the rod and reel, to see how it was working.

I stood up and waved. "Renato," I called, glad to be wearing the black head scarf he had sold me which was flapping in the wind. "Come sit down by me, honey," I said as he came nearer, and was all at once right there, smiling at me.

"I'm on my lunch hour," he told me. "I took the trolley. How do you like the fishing line?"

"Oh, honey, it's a good one." I reeled my line in to show him. "Nice and light and just suits me. But so far, it hasn't caught a thing."

He took it from me gently, then whipped it around, reminding me of my lost brother, Johnny, who used to fish just outside of Delcambre, Louisiana on the Vermilion River that fed into Vermilion Bay. I don't know that you could get there now.

Most of Mammy's family were fisher people or shrimpers who loved fishing and pulling in a good catch, and were happy and fun loving — Papa J's were more serious — who danced all night and sometimes to Cajun music or played cards for money on a big table in front of a wood stove where Mammy or one of the others — men and women — got up now and then to stir the fricassee, usually garden vegetables and shrimp or chicken in a stew.

Seems like Renato no more than had the line in the water when something was a-tugging and before you knew it, he had brought out this little wiggling snapper, shaking salt water.

"This rod and reel is OK," he said before throwing the fish back in the bay.

If I had still lived down in my old rooming house near Myrna Teague we could have kept it and I could have Renato and Myrna Teague and Billy for dinner. That is, if we caught more fish to go with this one and if I shopped for a green and made corn bread or a biscuit or two.

But when he turned to face me, I saw Renato looked so serious. I touched his shoulder.

"Renato," I asked, "what is the matter?"

He didn't look like a boy ought to look on his lunch hour. He told me then he was worried about his little brother, Julio.

"Julio didn't get a job this summer like he did last year for the newspaper." Then he paused. "He seems different."

"How is that, honey?"

He just shrugged, then said, "I hope he's not mixed up with the wrong people for easy money. He's just fifteen. Our father left a long time ago and our mother died. She never had a strong heart, like her parents before her. When she died they were already gone, and her relatives scattered in San Antonio and Houston and other places. (I guess just about all over Texas.) So Jesus and I have had to be mother and father, brother and sister since all of those are gone."

That was a lot for him to tell me, but I knew I had his trust from the hour when he walked me to the tackle store and then to the trolley. He said his family had lost people to cocaine dealers — and worse, crack — and to using, too. Some they knew the particulars on and some they didn't, but they mourned them all, even those they didn't like. He thought most had not been members of gangs.

"Julio has Jesus and me, so they won't get him. God only knows what happened to half of the family, to those who have moved away, uncles and cousins."

When he said this, looking right at me, I understood our connection — we needed each other. I needed a guide in the late twentieth century Corpus Christi. And he needed someone from a simpler time who would understand to tell this to.

"Honey," I said, "you are a worry wart. No reason to think just because Julio acts a little peculiar that Julio is in bad trouble."

"No," he said, handing my rod and reel back to me, "and I don't want him to be." Corpus Christi, he said, had some people who promised easy money. Maybe South Texas towns always had; after all, drug running took our Johnny.

"Darlin'," I told him, "the world is split right through. Poor people on the biggest part of it and greedy ones on the little strips that make up the other and Old Man Cruelty crossing over." I was about to mention what Leeland always said about this, when a car that I took for a very old Caddy with Julio in it came down the street and pulled into the T-head parking area where a few tourists were milling. I knew it was Julio because Renato called out his name. A few minutes later a boy who was stockier than Renato and shorter, but not much younger-looking, came toward us.

Wanted to know if he could borrow money.

"Just twenty dollars," he said. "I've got a hot tip on the dog races."

I had heard Corpus Christi had a big greyhound track not too far from the Bells' old neighborhood on the road to San Antonio in the back part of town.

Renato said, "I don't stand on my feet all day so you can gamble away my twenties."

"Honey," I asked after Renato had introduced me, "what is the dog's name?"

But Julio, who seemed a sullen boy, mad at the world about his condition, just shook his head and wouldn't tell me.

So I spoke again, "I might bet on a lucky dog," I told him. I knew from the way Renato looked at me it was the wrong thing to say.

God knew I should stay away from gambling. All a track ever brought me was a no good man and the wrong last name.

"I'm not going to lose," Julio said. "This tip is hot. I won't lose your twenty."

Oh, life is loss, honey! Something urged me to tell him. But I kept my mouth shut. Just loss. Loss. No matter what happens to that money. That's what I wanted to say.

Renato, who had drawn in the fishing line, slipped his hand in his pocket and took out his wallet. "I want this back," he said as he took out a twenty.

And Julio took it from him and said, "I promise you, you'll have your money." Then ran, without even giving me a nod, back to his long, black car.

Renato whipped the fishing line back into the water, mad at himself, I could see, for giving in to his baby brother.

"You probably did the right thing," I told him (but in my heart, I didn't think so). "He may really win something with that money."

Renato pulled the line in then and gave the rod back to me. Shrugged, gave me a pat on the arm and a smile.

"Keep in touch," he said. "You know where to find me."

A few moments later I heard him call, "Good luck to you with the fishing!" and I watched him step on a trolley and wave as it took off.

From the Seawall: Five

Poor Renato! He wanted a comfortable life for his baby brother, a life with no pain. Whether we like it or not, suffering goes on though, of course, we must try to stop it. Stop the worst of it. That's what I wanted to tell him. And that most of us aren't improved by it. We're not like the saints, or Jesus. We aren't improved one whit.

Anyway, that's my opinion and it was sometimes Elizabeth's, too. Elizabeth said her grandmother was a good example of a person who was not improved by suffering and that there were other outstanding examples in the family. Made most of them mean, she said, just as it did some sick people and most prisoners and so many outcasts and underdogs.

"But, once in a while," she told me, "some people become more compassionate as a result of having suffered, or at least learn more than most how to get through it." She wanted to know what I thought about that.

I said I couldn't say anything about whole groups of people, only particular cases.

"Well," she said, "let's talk about you, Aunt Rena. You lost your sister, Lucy, and your brother, Johnny, and your baby, Juliette, and years after that, Searcy's little boy who you looked after. And before you even grew up you married a man who was bad to you, and afterwards your baby died and you couldn't have another. And after you married Uncle Leeland who drank too much because, or so everyone says, he couldn't fulfill his dreams of building, and came to live with his not so happy family, you lost him, too. But you most always have a good time. If you can only talk about particular cases, tell me about you. Tell me, how do you stay happy?"

"Where do you want me to start?" I asked her. I didn't know what to say. As bad as I felt when I lost those people and as much as I missed them, Leeland most of all, happiness was just in me, like trees and grass and oceans and rivers are in the world.

"Start with your first big loss," she told me. "With your baby's death and then your little sister, Lucy's. Tell me how you got through that and then through Johnny's running away. And about the loss of Mammy and your daddy."

"Everyone loses her parents," I told Elizabeth, "and I was grown up before Papa J's death came, so while I grieved for a time, and I grieved for Mammy as much as for me, I got through it, and I believe we all did, by telling as much as any of us could remember about Papa J, about the time he cussed out the elders of the Presbyterian church when they stopped by the house to scold him for his poor church attendance — and to ask for money! Papa J was a quiet man who lived a quiet life, so we didn't have many dramatic stories."

But help came from telling any kind. About the way he plowed his field, following a tape line to keep the furrow straight. Can you imagine that? That way of plowing was particular to him. I never knew anyone else who did it. Or about the time we saw him break out in tears when he heard about a typhoid epidemic in a nearby parish on the radio news. He had lost a sister to typhoid, and although he wouldn't live to know it here, he would lose Lucy to typhoid, too.

Talking about the way Papa J was and what we liked in him, and even what we didn't, helped. (He was too quiet, honey, kept too much to himself, was distant from us.)

But Lucy! Lucy! For a long time I couldn't talk about her. (And words mean so much, darling.) In the beginning was The Word. Lucy, like her name, had the power to heal through the word that ran through her. From the time she was very small, those who were sick felt better when they just came near her, and some claimed to be healed by her touch, and maybe so, but even more I think were healed by what she said. And what was that?

"Do you know you are good with flowers? Do you know you help things grow? What do you care about those old school subjects?"

Honey, Lucy healed through The Word. What she gave was praise!

But she gave honest praise. Praised people for what they truly were or could do.

After she left us I couldn't much speak. Couldn't talk about Lucy, who died before she was twenty, pulled down into water and darkness — honey, for a long time I couldn't speak of her, or anything much. I sank into darkness, too.

But then I began to see her sometimes, and told myself that she would come back, that she wouldn't just go off and leave us without her forever.

"I will not leave you comfortless." Mammy always quoted Jesus saying that, but not until after Lucy died and then appeared many times before us, did I realize that the comforter he was talking about was not separate from us, but in us, in our power from all creation and in our connection to that.

And as time went on, I began to see that loss is part of living, though as often as not, unexpected. But that unexpected gifts, even after those who bring them are gone, arrive sometimes, too.

After awhile I saw how parts of life fit together the way I do when I work my crossword puzzles, looking for certain pieces that turn up sometimes only after I have been really still, really patient.

After maybe sitting at the table and staring at it, twisting a piece of my hair, all but memorizing the shapes of the pieces before me for maybe half a day. After I all but give up — look away from the mess before me and out the window at a jay sitting on an oak branch — just the right part will leap up at me, give me more of the picture, let me know it was worth it to sit in my chair by the table all day.

The one that turns up, I guess, is never the one we were expecting. I wasn't expecting Leeland. Or love. Or a child.

The last thing I thought when I married Leeland was that I would know the pleasure of caring for a child, have the friendship of a child, through him. But companionship and a lot of friendship from the little one I looked after came with her, along with some education, for Elizabeth taught me (even as I was teaching her), as children so often do.

From the Seawall: Six

As a grown person, I first learned from Searcy who showed me his need. Over and over he asked me to tell him about his mother and to get out the shoe box that held her pictures. So that one day I said to him, "I tell you what — why don't we do something with these pictures besides keep them in this box. Why don't we go to town and pick out a nice photo album to put them in? You can pick it out."

When we got to Kress's, Searcy spied a gold album more expensive than the rest. Though I don't know that he went to it because of its color, he picked it up first thing and asked, "Can we buy this one, Aunt Rena?" And though money was short, I decided that we could.

What a radiant boy he was by the time we got home! He never looked more like his mother, glowed all over, just shone. And going through the shoe box to select pictures for each page in the album absorbed him, took up the time when before he had moped or sulked around on rainy Saturday afternoons.

One or two of the pictures were bigger and more beautiful than the rest. In one, Lucy, in a blue dress, looking like the Mother of God, held Searcy in her arms, and in another Searcy and Johnny Two in their Sunday suits, sat either side of her. These pictures, we decided, needed featuring in the album. One in the front, maybe. One in the back. We couldn't decide where.

"I'll tell you what." I said, "why don't we just leave these two out."

"Leave them out?" Searcy asked.

"Yes," I told him. "We need to make another trip to Kress's. This time to look for frames."

As things turned out, one was all we needed. A double. And like our album, also gold.

The next I can remember learning from another person, who also happened to be a child I had cared for, was when Elizabeth made it clear that she was going to be away for a long time, away from me as well as the rest of her family. Maybe for the rest of her life. And that

I might not get to be with her during much of any of it.

And where did that happen? Would you believe it? In Kress's! I can be specific about the time and place, because one summer afternoon when I walked into Kress's and saw Elizabeth talking to her friend at the jewelry counter — he was a gay boy she went to school with, darlin', a Mexican Italian boy, as I may have mentioned, that times being what they were then, very few in Elizabeth's class had anything to do with or could accept. But in a different way, Elizabeth was also outside the status quo, and her Uncle Bo, too, so she and the boy, Bartola, as they called him, could talk about that. (I thought of him first thing when I came back to Corpus Christi and went into Kress's and saw Renato selling scarves.) On this particular day, I viewed Elizabeth in an entirely new way. I don't know exactly what made me see this — Elizabeth had been home all summer, working a typing job at the old Nueces Hotel and living with us to save a little money (oh, she planned to go back East, all right) after being in New York for a couple of years, and was nearly twenty and I was used to seeing her. I saw her every day — but when I first spied her with her friend on this day I saw her all at once as a grown woman, not our little girl anymore, and I saw that when she left this time it would be for good.

Did you ever do that, darlin'? Realize something important in a flash? And just know that it's right? I've done that once or twice and this was surely one of those times.

When I came close to Elizabeth I saw she had been crying, her eyes a little red and her pancake make-up streaked with tears. Then she held up her right hand, illuminated by all the colors of the rainbow under the fluorescent lights, and I saw her birthstone, a big garnet — I knew she had always wanted one, though she usually spent her savings on something else. Plane tickets, typewriters. Tape recorders and books.

"Look, Aunt Rena!" she said. "Look what Bartola has given me."

This was the first time I had met the boy, though she had told me some about him, about how she admired him for being himself and not trying to hide who he was.

"Bartola, this is my Aunt Rena."

"Do you like Elizabeth's ring?" he asked me. "It's from a special line we now carry."

"Why, darlin'," I said, "it's beautiful."

And I told the truth about that square cut dark red stone set in a gold filigree. "It looks Victorian."

"Do you think so?" Bartola asked, his voice both husky and high. "Like an antique?"

"Just like that," I said. "But it's bold."

The boy had given her a bold emblem of herself, that was clear to me immediately, though I wouldn't have said anything about it then. The message seemed to be: claim your life. (Just the way I had always encouraged her.) Go wherever you have to go.

She was gone for good shortly after that, darlin'.

When we got back to the house that night, Elizabeth told me that Bartola had plans of leaving for California.

"Pretty soon," I said, "we'll have no young people here. I sure hope you can get back for the holidays and to celebrate your birthday." (She didn't and I didn't see her again for twenty-five years.) I always liked to bake a cake on New Year's Eve for Elizabeth. As I may have mentioned, she was born on the same date I departed the world, one minute after midnight, on a January 1.

No, Elizabeth didn't get home that year for Christmas or her birthday and somehow I even lost track of where she was. She traveled, darlin'. But I knew I would always be a part of her life, no matter where it took her, just as she was of mine.

When she was a grown woman, she wrote me a letter that said, "Aunt Rena, the final condition of my childhood which turned out to be the foundation that supports and sustains me, rested on you."

All my life, even after I stopped hearing very much from Elizabeth, who became a wanderer, I kept that letter, and I asked Searcy to keep it after me with the idea of giving it to her maybe if she ever showed up for a visit or if one of us found out where she had finally gone.

I heard she had gone West, but not until she came to see me years later in Shreveport, a middle-aged woman, darlin', did I realize that "West" meant California, which had always seemed to me beyond the west, the other side of the west (or, at any rate, surely the last of it). Whether she stayed there or not, I don't know. What happened to her after that last time that I saw her, I don't know.

Elizabeth was a questioner and a seeker, always quoted Jesus on that, and made me realize that, by nature I was, too. Maybe Johnny had encouraged me to be, and maybe reaching out, even when it wasn't safe, was just in our blood, mine and Johnny's — in some ways Johnny always seemed an older me, a male me, and a guide. But when I was young I didn't think about this much (just knew it somewhere deep inside).

From the Seawall: Seven

When Elizabeth was a very little girl, she used to tickle me by looking right at me and asking, "Aunt Rena, who are you?" Just as the wind asks me here.

"Elizabeth," I would tell her, "once I was just Rena Brock from Louisiana, the southern part near Vermilion Bay. Once I was a round-faced blue-eyed girl with curly black hair I never had to fix much — a blessing, darling — though I pulled it off my face when I grew old. For a long time, though, it curled all around it. Once I was no older than you!" She would laugh and laugh when I said that.

I went on to say our mama told stories to us when we were children, but then grew quieter and farther from us. That's what life does, takes us away from the very ones we gave life to. Took Mammy away from us children finally. But we knew she loved us: she never whipped any of us, never scolded. Smiled at us all the time, the Louisiana sun in her and even more of it in Lucy who healed some of the arthritic, crippled people she came near. Wrapped herself around the legs of an old crippled man who brought her peppermint when she was only two. And when she let go, his legs straightened and he walked as good as any of us.

Johnny, our big brother, brought sunshine, too. Never mind that we found out he was running drugs across the border. Where did he go? That was the question I asked after he slipped into Mexico.

The Bells weren't sunny. The Bells are another story. When I married Leeland I saw how they were different, how they weren't a family who laughed much or who touched one another, funny people, I thought, that way.

Lord, you have to hold your children! Tell them how beautiful they are.

Although I knew Ellen Bell didn't like me (but that it was nothing personal), and that she had hurt her own children, I tried to feel affection for her because she was Leeland's mother, and I came to. She said cutting things about people. Hard on them! But a lot of the time she was just silent and fretted, working her brow to and fro, I expect hard on herself, too. I could see the worry in her and it was easier to care for her then. Her family had been stern with her and with her brothers and sisters as she was with her own children. Hard on them, cruel even (part of that came out of the religion), the same way. Leeland from the beginning grew closer to his daddy than to his mother, pretty young separated himself from her.

Hard on children! What a thing for any of us to be.

Give children tenderness and they'll grow up tender. Childhood for Lucy and Johnny and me was happy. Later on, Papa J died (but his death came quick and brought no pain.) Then Johnny ran away and into Mexico. So life got sadder. Never sadder than when I married that first time except later on when I lost my baby and then a long time later in life lost Searcy's little boy. And finally lost Leeland. But I had to find him first! So I knew joy. Became one of the lucky ones who knew joy, too.

I met Leeland in a blackberry thicket one steaming summer day. He and Daddy Bell were in Louisiana building bridges, one of them across the Texas-Louisiana line. I hadn't spoken with him for more than a few minutes when I knew he would be the one for years and years. But why was that? And how did I know it? Oh, I wonder, darling.

I had been picking berries on a day like this one, July and sweltering, had a bucket full when I remembered the tributary to the river that ran nearby. Then I put my bucket down and slipped out of the berry thicket and at the riverbank out of my cotton dress, and wearing only a chemise and panties, slipped into the water, cool because it was flowing, and shaded by big trees. I swam down deep and stayed under, eyes open, looking at the pretty pebbles of blue and gray and rose, and when I came up I saw a tall, thin man bent over the bank smiling at me.

I ducked under again right away and swam back to the bank I had left. In swimming I lost myself, found release. But I had to do it alone. I heard the splash he made into the water and I swam fast for my dress on shore, but when I came up for air not too far from it, this long white man with freckled arms and sweet thin lips (they always seemed to be smiling, darlin') swam beside me.

"Fine swimmin' hole, ain't it?" he said.

The "ain't" I could tell was put on.

"I have to get out," I told him. "I've left off blackberry picking."

As I touched the bank, he asked, "What's your name?"

"Rena," I said it plainly. Stood all but nude before him, oddly glad of it, dripping wet, happy, my chemise sticking to my breasts. Then, all at once shy, I threw my dress over my head and ran dripping into the thicket, thrashing through the berries, the trees just loaded with them, their shapes making patterns on my light frock, staining the gauzy fabric on it so that I could never wear it again except to scrub a floor or to can or cook in. But I knew I would never throw it away.

And when I came to the place where I had been picking those overripe berries, plump, glossy (oh, so sweet, darlin'), Leeland soon stood beside me, telling that he didn't mean any disrespect, but that he wanted to get to know me.

"What makes you think you do?" I asked him.

He blushed and grinned. Later he told me he could see I took pleasure where I found it.

"I like a woman who is at home in the out of doors, isn't embarrassed to jump in some water when she's hot." He added that he was a builder and outside all the time. Then he looked down at my full bucket. "I see you've a mess of blackberries."

A serious aspect to Leeland. He meant what he said. Wasn't just being fresh or smart.

"Well," I said, "do you like a blackberry cobbler?"

I wanted to be with him all the time from the start, and invited him and his daddy — after I learned his daddy was with him and that both of them camped near the bridge site — to our house for the Fourth of July. Although I had not until that moment once ever thought about it, I said we planned to have catfish and gumbo fillet with blackberry cobbler for dessert.

And, darlin', it was a good party. After we said hello, he introduced his daddy, who was, I could tell right away, a person who liked to laugh some. Though he had a serious aspect and some darkness was in him — and in us all, darlin' — sunshine shot through him, too.

We had our fish and our gumbo and after supper, Leeland pulled out a bunch of plans out of a cracked leather valise he had with him, said he wanted me to see them if I wouldn't mind looking and right after, spread them all out on the floor. And when he did I saw everything come over him, excitement and pain — passion, honey, with all the torment — and all the sweetness — that can be in that. I didn't know anything about architecture, or about building, but as I sat there beside Leeland that night as he pointed out the difference in the design of two big bridges, and to the rooms of a ranch style church he meant to put up for the Catholics near Nacogdoches (my funeral service was conducted in it, honey), I knew I would learn something about it because it consumed this man. And after he died I spent weeks poring over his plans trying to see the way he had made them. And, if truth be known, darlin', trying to find him in one of his rooms.

When he had been gone awhile and I still couldn't, I took off for Acapulco and when that trip was over, and after I took up with, then got rid of that no good Dubuffet, I traveled in Mexico some more. I don't know, maybe I was still looking for Johnny. Or maybe I was deranged and thought I might find Leeland. Whatever the reason, I drove my old car, a De Soto Leeland bought one time after his old Studebaker would no longer go, drove it out of Arkansas down the South Texas coast and into Mexico where I had gone by train when I was a girl. Maybe I thought I would enter another dimension if I just drove on.

To tell you the truth, Leeland often seemed so near that I think I believed that the place where he was overlapped whatever place I was in.

Anyway, after he died, the next world seemed just over the Texas state line — if it was that far. And I didn't expect it to be much different. (Mexico never seemed much of a foreign country.) On the other side of Laredo I followed the winding road into the mountains all the way to Monterrey, and after I spent some weeks there, Myrna Teague joined me as I had called and asked her (she used some of her insurance money and took a plane on down) and the two of us followed another road to the city where Bo Bell once wanted to live. Tampico. (I don't know why Bo was stuck on that — he just wanted to live in a place where he felt freer — and think maybe he had just looked on a map down the coast of Mexico and picked out a name.)

When I traveled in Mexico, I felt a little better driving the roads with Myrna along, though driving in the Mexican countryside is not really safe for even two women together to do. Finally, we turned west into the interior. Looking back, I see we took some awful chances. Not that I ever considered Mexico romantic. Not even when I was young, and I ran off into it in that wild way after my baby died. I expected something different, darlin'. But I always knew it was a poor country and hard to live in, that it was easy to get sick, or I had heard, attacked by bandits or (if you were a young girl), sold into prostitution, or even to get thrown into prison for something you didn't do. I had heard all the stories, darlin', and knew some of them were true. But I also knew Johnny had gone there, and I thought maybe even after all the years that had passed since he fled, I would hear something of him or even find some trace.

In the evening in the *zocalos* when I watched the boys and girls promenade past one another, I more than ever, remembered Johnny and Lucy as children. And after Myrna joined me, thought I saw each of them once or twice — first in Veracruz, then in Jalisco (I'll tell you about that soon).

After Myrna left me — she had a round trip ticket — I headed back, drove all the way back up into Texas and Corpus Christi where Myrna was and where Elizabeth was, by this time, living with Daddy and Ellen Bell and with her mama's and Leeland's baby brother, her uncle Bo. I figured I would just drop in. I would surprise them, and stay for the afternoon and maybe, through supper, or even, if they had room and I felt welcome, for a day or two. I pulled into the driveway in the back of the house, right in front of the garage apartment, early on a sultry Sunday morning. Elizabeth, who was cutting roses, all those dark ones Bo grew (they were nearly black, darlin'), was the first to see me. Dropped the scissors and came running for the gate, all arms and legs, a gangly thing. And threw her arms around me still clutching the roses. I knew when I saw her that, if I could, I would stay until she finished high school. She seemed almost my child.

A few minutes later Bo seemed happy to see me and later on in the morning said he would be glad to have me stay on the property with the family, said I could live in the garage apartment while

Elizabeth's mama and stepfather, who was on a traveling job for Tennessee Gas, were away, and in the spare room next to Ellen's if they came back for a visit.

Two or three years later after Elizabeth graduated from high school and was on her way into her own troubled life (nobody's is trouble-free, darlin'), I didn't know just where I should go.

Searcy often wrote and told me to come back to Louisiana, and I did that for awhile, lived in Shreveport where Searcy moved after he remarried, and to please him, in a little house in town. But finally all of Louisiana seemed strange to me. I had been in my late twenties when I married Leeland and left it.

One day in the early spring of Elizabeth's graduation year when I saw the first wild flowers, primroses and bluets (those deep blues!) just cropping up in the grass, I knew that what I should do if I followed my heart, was go back to the country Leeland liked so much in East Texas, the other side of Nacogdoches. Leeland loved that country, best of all the Texas country because of its trees which reminded him of the Ouachita woods in his native Arkansas. I knew I would be happy living in a place he loved. And at the same time I would be close enough to Searcy to visit when I liked (he had remarried, darlin', a quiet girl I wanted to get to know) and set my foot back on childhood's home.

And, of course, finally, that's what I did. Left Shreveport where Elizabeth as a middle-aged woman visited me once, the very last time I saw her. Just moved into a little house near Nacogdoches and planted a garden. I hadn't been there long when Searcy and his wife left Louisiana, not to return for a year or two, and moved nearby.

Finally, I had to live with them. (Searcy took me to Louisiana for burial after my funeral in the Catholic church that Leeland built.) But we stayed in East Texas until I died.

But when Elizabeth was in high school, I knew it wasn't time to leave Corpus Christi, so I just went on there, and as much as I could, tried to help Bo out in the house and yard. Paid my way, too, bought a lot of groceries for us out of my Social Security.

Daddy was still living when I first came and I saw him through his last sickness, and Mother Bell through hers. Both died of cancer, darlin', he of the face, she of the colon and in agony, went out screaming with the pain.

Daddy, though, was at peace toward the end, hugged Elizabeth and kissed Ellen and told her good-bye. And asked all of us if we saw Leeland who he said was sitting on the foot of the bed.

Before he found that peace and that reunion with his oldest son, he had done some suffering, I can tell you, and he sunk into a long coma toward the end. For two days before he died we could all hear the death rattle from as far away as the street. Daddy had lain on his bed on the sun porch through most of the days and nights since the beginning of his sickness, the cancer daily growing bigger and spread all across his face. He asked Elizabeth to paint it with the green medicine the doctor left and told the rest of us that he wanted only her to do it because she had the gentlest touch.

Through it all, he was a good patient, seldom complained, and darlin', I know he hurt. He never asked for extra attention. Was interested in Elizabeth's progress at school and in her friends and comings and goings. And when she came in from dates and parties — often through the back door, honey, and his bed was there in the back room, back on the sun porch — he would call out to her and sit up in his bed and talk to her and ask her if she had a good time.

Sometimes when that boy Elizabeth liked so much brought her home — he was a new boy in town, from out of state, Kansas and half Jewish, somebody said — I would hear him and her whispering out on the porch under or near the bougainvillea vine, could hear him say, "Think about it, Elizabeth." (For months he had been asking her to go steady.) And could hear her breathin', "I will, Ben." Seems I could all but hear her hands sliding up the silky material of whatever shirt he was wearing, the little kisses he planted all over her face. (Maybe I was just remembering Leeland and me together.) And then would hear her tiptoe into the house — hear Daddy softly calling to her to ask her if she had been to a dance or party and if she had had a good time. And she would always say, "Yes, I did, Grandaddy. How are you feeling?" And he would always say, "I'm just fine."

Oh, but his sore got bigger and bigger and spread across his face and down across his throat — no medicine the doctor gave him could stop it. And one afternoon he asked for us to wire Elizabeth's mama who was off with her husband, Bud, on one of his jobs, to come home if they could. He wanted to see her, he said, and believed his time to do that was growing short. (He hadn't been able to eat in a long time — just a little soup from a spoon.) And so Elizabeth wrote out the wire and took it to the Western Union.

Daddy sank back on his bed as soon as he knew she had done it. And the death rattle began right after.

Have you ever heard a death rattle?

Honey, I'm telling you, it's a fierce sound, deeper than the reptile kind — and Daddy's was loud; no stop, no pause to it. Made an awful music, and I expect fell into the big whirring noise of the universe, maybe even came out of and finally fit back into the hideous roar of that. (Why "hideous?" Oh, I don't know. I guess most of us just aren't up to hearing it. I wish I could tell you, darlin'.) At any rate, for more than thirty-six hours, it just went on and on.

Made me nervous sure enough. We were all of us all that day pacing around, walking out into the yard on any excuse. I said I was going to pull weeds from the flower beds (a job that in heat I hated) or to edge grass. In the evening I went out to water — and that was more pleasant, and to cut roses and gardenias so we would have cut flowers in the house when the doctor came. The doctor said he could hear the death rattle over the phone when Bo called and said he didn't believe the end could be too far.

And we all agreed it would be a blessing.

But the doctor was wrong. The rattle went on all through the long, hot night. A steady whir, a persistent drumming I thought of as African. Whirra, whirra, whirra and then, Ram! Ram! Ram! I kept getting up to go out for some air. Even though there wasn't any. Or very little. And what there was, hot, and smelled of gas.

I slept a little toward morning, but of course, woke up feeling sick and groggy. Although it was only May I could tell we were going into more heat and another brutal day.

And the death rattle went on through it until Elizabeth's Mama got there.

Stopped as soon as she walked into the room. Daddy pulled himself up on the bed, sat bolt upright and looked around as normal as you please.

And said then, "Thank God," as he hugged his only girl, and Bud, and Elizabeth, and finally, Bo and me. And then called out for Ellen, crying, "Ellen, you see what faith can do." And kissed her on the cheek.

And then he asked us if we could see Leeland. (And, of course, we couldn't.) Told us positively that Leeland was right there with us.

"Do you see Leeland there?"

I looked toward what I hoped would be him, or at least for some something luminous around the place that should be him, for at least a circle of light.

No one answered. Not one of us saw him. Or anything.

Then Daddy said, "Well, he's right here." He pointed toward the folded quilt that covered his feet. "I don't know why you don't see him." Daddy sounded annoyed with all of us. "He's sitting right on the foot of the bed."

I was jealous then of Daddy Bell's dying (could have put up with terrible suffering and all if that's what it took to do it), of his positive belief that Leeland was with him. Honey, my faith wasn't strong.

All during this time I watched Elizabeth grow into herself and when she had time at home, I enjoyed her company. And as you know, I enjoyed riding the buses. And visiting with my friend Myrna Teague who liked to talk about our Mexican travels, and Billy Park, and yes, Bill Powers. And talking to various ones. To whoever would hear me or just to the wind, or just to myself and to nobody else at all.

Churches

Photo by Daryl Bright Andrews

Churches

Renato caught the morning's only fish. I caught memory and a glimpse just before I left, of Lucy's face rising above the water, her dark face shining, and her mouth open, lips moving — oh, I thought she would speak! — as if she had something to say.

And I asked aloud: "Are you here to announce some news?"

But heard nothing.

And I left the seawall after that.

Turned once to wave to Lucy. But when I did, she was gone. So I walked to the trolley which took me back to the Ramada Inn and, from there, took a city bus to the Catholic church on top of the bluff which had a sign that said:

COME IN STOP REST PRAY

The door was locked or, honey, I would have done it. So I decided to walk on. The heat was bad; this was July and it was near a hundred. So I went very slow. I even took a chance and walked across a freeway that hadn't been there thirty years before, and surprised me. Although when I started out it hadn't a car on it, I worried I wouldn't make it all the way across without being run down by something that might come from out of the blue.

But it was a day on which not much was moving. So I made it, lifting my skirt, to step over the railing in the middle, and went on. I walked all the way to the Presbyterian. Oh, I was slow, honey. It was a longer walk than I had remembered and took a long time and the heat was terrible. Because the churches were so far back from the bay and the seawall, the bluff raised over that, they got less wind. Wind would have cooled me, darlin', but it also might have toppled me over.

On my way I passed the YW where I stayed once years ago and where I thought I might stay again the next time I came to Corpus Christi. (I wasn't thinking then that the next time I came I wouldn't need a room.) Maybe I could have a hot plate so that if I caught a good fish I could cook and eat it. By the time I got to the church the sweat was dripping off of me, running down my legs and I could feel my old heart beating. Could hardly get my breath.

Now, as I told you, because Mammy was Catholic and Papa J Presbyterian, I went to church both places when I was growing up, though not every Sunday, and I never learned much about the differences and never cared. Prayer is prayer, honey, no matter where you do it, and no matter who you are, it finds its way. In my last years in Nacogdoches when I went to church at all I went to the Catholic — there was only one small one for the whole county — and never mind that I was a divorced woman, several times a divorced woman. (Wonder why I kept the name of that no good man, Dubuffet?) People in that church looked more like the ones I knew when I was a girl in Louisiana, didn't wear as many sober expressions as they did in the Presbyterian, and anyway, I had always loved the Mass.

But here in Corpus Christi the Presbyterian looked so pretty, friendly even, that I wanted to go in it. Oh, the Presbyterian seemed fine! But would you believe it was also locked, honey? What kind of world do we live in when we can't even get in the churches? I didn't know, but since I couldn't, I just stood by the door and got my breath and said a prayer and sat down on the steps for awhile until my heart stopped beating so hard. (You know your heart is beating too hard when you can feel it.)

And when I got up, I walked down the long block some more — this was the longest walk I had just about ever taken, and I was past ninety, darlin'. If a car had passed by I would have called out to it. But on that ghost street no car came.

Then I neared The Good Shepherd, an Episcopal church that looked Catholic because of the Spanish architecture and what had been cream colored stucco, gray now in places and in need of a good cleaning — where I all at once remembered Elizabeth when she was in high school used to go. The church back then had been new and pretty. Though they had been brought up Methodist, Elizabeth took her mother and Bo to The Good Shepherd — she loved the Episcopal church partly because it was the one where Leeland took her when she was small (he left her in a Sunday school there two doors from a club where he could drink if he brought his own bottle) — and I believe both were confirmed Episcopalians though neither went often. Except for Ellen, none of the Bells were faithful churchgoers, and I always thought Ellen went mostly so she could dress up.

Anyway, when I found myself in front of The Good Shepherd I was dizzy, sure enough, faint. I told myself that after I rested on the steps, I would try to find someone in the rectory — I saw it across the street — and use the phone to call a taxi to take me back to my motel on Shoreline. And never mind what the driver charged! But, to my surprise, I found that when I tried the door to the church, it was open, and that made me so happy that I just stepped inside.

I sat down in one of the pews in back and it felt so good to do that, to be in air conditioning and out from under the broiling sun, that I hardly noticed what was going on. I didn't sink down into the wine-colored cushion meant for kneeling — couldn't, honey — but just bowed my head for a minute. I knew God and all the angels would forgive me for not kneeling and that so would most of the people who stared.

When I entered, a young man who I guessed was an usher whispered, "Take that place there, Mother," and nodded at the empty space at the last pew's end.

Why had he called me "Mother?" Just because of my age, I guessed. (To my disappointment, a mother was something I hadn't been for long.) I didn't know, just smiled at him and sat. And that felt so good I was afraid I might never get up.

The church was packed and I had taken one of the few empty places. As I sat there, sweat pouring down my back and over the sag of my breasts, and down my legs, my dress sticking to me — and this with the air-conditioning on (and that sure felt good, honey!), I thought it was odd, a little peculiar, that so many people had turned out at noon on a Thursday to take Communion and pray. I thought it must be a saint's day, but I never knew saints were so popular with Episcopalians. I tried to remember what the saints' days for July were but, except for Mary Magdalene, I couldn't think of one.

As I sat there wondering and cooling down, the minister took the pulpit and spoke of this being another kind of Easter service. What did he mean? I felt sorry for Mary Magdalene then, for her grief.

Poor Mary M. Had the church decided to give her Easter, her own Easter in July? I imagined her as small. I thought of her rolling away the heavy stone, maybe in terrible heat. I knew Jesus loved her. Easter, this is like another Easter, the minister had said. Hot, for Easter, I thought. Even for a different kind. Maybe I had walked in on a sermon which would teach me something, open a window on a new world.

Then it hit me.

I had come to someone's funeral.

I was glad I still had on the big black scarf that Renato had sold me tied around the back of my head, glad I was still wearing the dark blue dress which I had rinsed out in the sink the night before (filthy from the bus ride, honey), and not the red one, the other dress I had with me, but which on account of the heat and Searcy's lecturing me against wearing such a color, I had almost left at home. Most people, I noticed, were in black though a few around me wore white or gray. But some were just in dark colors. (I always thought white was nice for a funeral and wanted to wear it when Leeland died, but Ellen Bell discouraged me.)

The person who died was named Joe. I remembered that Elizabeth when she was in middle life, in the last year I saw her, had cared for a man named Joe. And that he had died. He was someone she had worked with or for, an old broadcaster she admired. He was married — "well married," I remember she had said that — so that they could only be friends, with some thread of romance maybe between them. And she had said also something profound. I never knew what — maybe some inkling of eternity, darlin'; I had the idea from listening to her that it had to do with intuitions about whatever it is in us that lasts. But I wasn't straight on that (who is?), only clearly knew that the friendship meant a lot to Elizabeth who never really connected to anybody in flesh. She never married, never even lived with anybody outside her family. Like her Uncle Bo that way, and a sadness to her, darlin'. And to me for her. Ellen Bell's legacy. In some ways she was like my child. Who would have thought she would have a life like that?

I said a prayer for Joe whose funeral I attended as if he was Elizabeth's friend. Or my own beloved.

"Joe's family is happy now," the minister said. "They know he is well taken care of and in the best place."

72

Please welcome Joe, I said in my prayer. Please treat him right. Make him feel at home and forgive any meanness he was into or did here. (All of us sometimes have meanness in our hearts.) Lies he told. Betrayals. Ease his people's grief.

"Joe's family," he went on, "should be happy now for he's all right!"

When you lose someone you love, it's damn hard to be happy. And I doubt that Joe's family was.

I remember when Ellen Bell's Methodist minister talked about Leeland "going to glory." When he said that, I wept bitter tears. Were they just selfish? Was Leeland better off all that long way from me?

"Ease their grief," I said that again. Aloud. Just as if Joe were my very own family. And in a sense I guess he was.

As the service went on, I thought maybe a lot of people ought to take up attending the funerals of strangers. Had Leeland sent me back to Corpus Christi so I could pray for Joe? Oh, honey, the dead need mourners! And the Bible tells us Jesus said, "Blessed are those who mourn." Well, Mary Magdalene was there for him. Bless her heart.

Maybe, I considered, Leeland had sent me to Corpus Christi so I would forever be a part of the power of Communion that joins us to everything and to one another. ("Galaxies," the prayer book said — I couldn't see the words, honey, but heard those around me say them, "suns, the planets in their courses, and this fragile earth, our island home." During this service the minister stumbled over, then repeated this part.) Maybe when I went back to East Texas I would attend more funerals. Joe of Corpus Christi had a lot of friends or at least a lot of connections for the church was full! But back where I had come from I knew some people died with only a handful of mourners. Or none at all. That was probably true, I told myself, in Corpus Christi, too.

Leeland hadn't had many. Because he drank, the Masons wouldn't attend. He once aspired to belong to them, even to attain the 32nd Degree, whatever that was, and I don't think he knew. If he had, might have hated whatever it was — he just wanted to belong to some order that he believed stood for right. To tell you the truth, at his funeral even I couldn't send any good word up to or for him. I just wanted him back, just wanted him there beside me. I didn't hear what the minister said.

I was numb, honey.

And I hurt so after. I was in pain, darlin'.

Pain, anyway, is the only word we have for what I was in, so I guess that's what I have to call it. I never remember feeling like that. Some asked me why I didn't cry. I couldn't have answered them. But now I know. Because it was too deep a hurt to let go of. So, for a long time I didn't.

Then one day I woke up and stood up and held onto a wall and tore a fingernail trying to pull that wall down around me. And then I heard an unearthly noise — and it was coming from me, darlin'. I didn't know what to make of it, but the neighbors told me I keened.

But then after a long time, months and months I think it was, I slept through a whole night and well into the morning and I woke up hungry. And this after a hundred days of hardly eating and nights when I barely slept at all, and oh, people said I looked thin and haggard. I can't tell you how I looked because I never saw myself, not even when I stood before a mirror. Darlin', I ghosted out in front of the glass.

But that morning I woke to the prophecy in my name come true: I was reborn. (When I was little, Mammy told me she named me Rena so I would never have to die.)

And so I dressed myself and walked to the nearest cafe and ordered grits and eggs and my old favorite, blackberry cobbler. And then I left the cafe and walked to the cafeteria and picked up bowls of slaw and fried eggplant and black-eyed peas and several kinds of greens. And sat down and ate them all. And then went back for strawberry shortcake. I should have been sick. But I wasn't. For months I hadn't been able to keep anything down. As they say, I could hardly swallow water. But when I woke up on this morning I was so hungry that I just ate my way through the whole day, tasted everything as if it was for the first time, devoured it. And it was all so good.

And when I looked at the world, it was as if I was seeing it for the first time — trees so green, sky so blue. Oh, yes, it was summer, darlin'! July and hot, wet with humidity, but also with sparkling. And I loved it.

"Thank you," I said out loud while walking down the street. "Thank you for the morning." I addressed the air — and who knows? — maybe in it the Holy Ghost.

"Hot," people said to me.

And I said, "Yes, I love it."

I wanted to go dancing that night.

Leeland loved to dance. No matter what he said about dancing, he loved it.

"The mouth is the instrument of mendacity." Leeland himself said that. "But the body doesn't lie."

When he and I were first married he and I would go to dances and sometimes danced all night. Did that, instead of, like some couples, going to picture shows. Leeland didn't think much of shows. And he got mad at me for liking some of them and sneaking off to matinees.

Most of the time we were too poor to go anywhere so we just stayed home and listened to the radio — no wonder Elizabeth wanted to write radio shows, she saw us around it so much listening to those sounds, as if the radio was magic. And, of course, it was. And is.

And the telegraph and telephone. And the way I can now talk to you! (Even though I have returned to what I think of as "dream time," or that is what I suppose.)

Sometimes we read stories aloud to one another. We read some of the good, exciting ones from the Bible like Esther's and Joseph's and the one in Matthew that told all the miracles that Jesus did. And we read some stories from a book of fables Leeland had. And some from mystery magazines. Leeland read all those to me, and oh, darlin', he was the mystery, who he was and why my life was entwined with his. (When I asked, he would say there was no reason, it just was.) Or we would play cards, Black Jack or Pitch — Daddy used to join us — and we had some good times doing that.

And in the night we made love, held each other and with so much longing and so many small kisses (and a few deep ones, darlin'), and wet all over and aching slipped into each other just right.

Then came the long year of Leeland's dying and that was hard to take. He wrote, just before he died, "I love you" on a piece of paper and I knew it was true. But, at the same time, it astonished me, always had, why it should be, why it ever was — that was the real mystery story. One day, I told myself, I have to find out. Then he wrote, "If I could only have a cup of coffee." I guess I told you he had cancer of the throat. Maybe from rolling and smoking all that Bull Durham and mixing it with so much whiskey. He couldn't speak.

After I came back to myself — and yet also to a new person — I just wanted to go out, to the nightclubs, go dancing. Shake Old Death away, shake, rattle and roll Old Death away.

I had a little money saved up from Leeland's insurance and winnings from the races and I bought some burgundy satin clothes. Oh, red was my color, honey. And the dark reds went with night!

When Jack Dubuffet saw me he thought I was a woman whose husband had left her money. He was thirty-nine and I was nearly fifty and ought to have known better, but he seemed sincere. Like an old time gentleman, that you read about in books (and maybe that's the only place they were). He was so pretty. And he could dance.

And I thought, oh, Lord, this is what I need in these years left to me. I've had all I want of what weighs heavy. Poverty and relations — and yes, love, too — and all that long dying. My life with Leeland was heavy with all of that. Jack Dubuffet might just like dancing.

Oh, I found out different.

I left him knowing for all the time left me, knowing for always, that I had been foolish to think I was going to have some lighthearted dancing years with a pretty man. When he found out I didn't have anything but a little Social Security and what was left of Leeland's insurance money — I lost most of it on the horse — he struck me with the back of his hand. And then with his fists, honey. And when that happened I knew that when he stopped I would dance alone or go to each dance for the rest of my dancing time, with a different fella. And that for awhile I wouldn't be going anywhere. (I couldn't dance, honey, could hardly get around.)

After I left him I didn't know what to do, as I guess I've told you — oh, darlin', I know I may get tiresome. Forgive me, but don't we

all repeat ourselves? Repeat, and repeat? So I just struck out for
Mexico — by that time, it had become a habit — drove down the
Texas coast right around Corpus Christi, didn't think to even ask
Myrna if she wanted to come along until I was all the way to
Monterrey. I guess, as I've said, deep inside, I thought maybe I would
at last find Johnny. Or who knows? Maybe Leeland's ghost. And
when I went as far into Mexico as I could and still didn't find either,
not really, not even with my friend Myrna Teague along, I turned
back and traveled the other way.

You were Rena Bell, I told myself. And are still Rena Bell even if
you now at the end of your name also have a Dubuffet. So go back
and live with the Bells who are still your people.

Oh, I knew Ellen Bell didn't like me, and Bo only some of the
time. (Sometimes he was influenced by his mother.) Still, I thought
that Leeland's family was the place for me, that I could help out
with all the dying and that by taking me in to do that, Ellen and
Daddy Bell would also help me. And that Elizabeth and I could be
together for a little while before she packed her bags for college.

Plain to see she was going to go, and I knew I had encouraged her
to get out of the house where there was so much sickness and anger,
where they all just worked all the time and stuck to one another,
where they would never let in anyone new.

"Life is too short," I told her, "for you to stay here. Get out and
find yourself some friends. Oh, there are a lot of nice people. You
can hardly take a bus ride without meeting them. Just introduce
yourself and begin. You know how. I see you do it. You aren't like
the Bells who cut themselves off.

"A long time ago something caught hold of them — oh, I don't
know what it was, and kept them away from life. "But it hasn't got
you, yet. You've learned something else. And everything you are
takes you the other way. Honey, go out beyond this family. Then you
can return when and if you want to."

"Aunt Rena," she said, "you went deep into Mexico."

And I told her, "Yes, but it never seemed to me a foreign country,
but like an extension of Texas, only going farther in."

For a long time so much of the country looked the same. Miles
and miles of plains, barren places, plenty of mesquite. But I did go

far in. And I came on mountains — you could only imagine mountains in our part of Texas — and trees and flowers the likes of which I had never seen. Women with baskets of roses — towers of roses! — on their heads in Oaxaca. And, for someone who had been a long time in Texas, other odd sights.

Myrna and I arrived in Oaxaca on a Friday and after we checked into our hotel just off the central plaza and washed up, we went right away into the big church on one side of that square, dark clouds banked all around it (though they never brought rain), and saw a man standing in front of the altar there in one of the side chapels for one of the saints, masturbating. His member out of his pants and his hand right on it, moving up and down.

Well, darlin', out of respect for whatever moment he was having, the love affair he was in — and, oh, that's what it was, in an instant I could see that — I tried to look away.

But Myrna whispered, "Do you see that?"

And I had to look back at him!

Later Myrna asked, "How could he desecrate the church that way?"

And I told her I didn't think he meant it as a desecration.

"I think maybe," I told her, "he is in an ecstasy."

I saw how communication with a saint could lead on to that. But Myrna didn't get this when I tried to tell her and she said it was a wonder to her he wasn't reported and arrested, not that she personally cared what anybody did.

She said, "I personally don't care what anybody does, but I don't think we should have to see this."

I agreed it was too bad he was on view. I thought maybe he ought to be able to pull a curtain. I thought I understood how he wanted to be transported, or nearly was — that he wanted out of himself, that he wanted union. We often want that when we pray, don't we? If we prayed with our whole selves, if we didn't just put our prayers in a separate chamber from the rest of us, if we didn't just keep them mental, maybe we'd all want to take our bodies with us when we made them (and in a way wanting to get out of those bodies that trap us into our separateness, too). What he was after seemed to me natural. But us looking at the way he had to do that was another thing! So I had to agree with Myrna about his exposure.

"Let's move on," I told her. "Let's just go on the other way."

Myrna told me once that although she cared for Mr. Teague, she never thought much of sex, not that she disliked it exactly, and didn't see why people made so much fuss.

"I don't see what all the fuss is about," she told me, "at least not for women. That's something men want to do much more than women."

(When she spoke, I could almost hear Ellen Bell whisper, "the nasty things!") I guess Myrna couldn't help not knowing about the pleasure and release. (Or maybe she did and, even though she was a straight shooter about most things, thought it would shame her to admit it.) Or Ellen either, who I expect had been brainwashed and maybe, even abused as a child. How many women did? And why was I so lucky? Because I grew up swimming rivers? Because in our family we all cared for each other with touch? Because, though they took me to Communion, I never went to Confession and until just a few days before I was married when I had to be instructed (and then most of it I didn't understand) no one in my family spoke to me about sin or any rules that went with church?

I enjoyed Myrna's company and she was modern in a lot of ways, what I called modern. After all, Mr. Teague left her nothing except life insurance and she took care of herself, clerking in stores and sometimes sewing for people, after he died. And, there was a streak of adventure in her; she liked having a good time with friends. Who else would have gone with me to Mexico? So I didn't make a case for the man we had seen playing with his member right there in the chapel of that big church. (Darlin', I believe it was a cathedral.) Not even when Myrna talked about him as if he was some kind of freak.

"Let's move on," I said, and we did.

But later in the afternoon in the place we had come to after wandering through many streets and seeing Indian women with long pigtails — down to their knees, darlin' — dancing in long, red and gold striped dresses and Indian children wearing capes embroidered with pictures of the Virgin chasing each other and playing tag, and many more in plain worn out clothes begging around tables where tourists were eating and drinking, we saw an old man, all in white, white shirt and pants, straw sandals and a big, natural colored sombrero — he was maybe seventy — at the side of another church in front of one of the statues and he was also exposed, erect and whacking. And moving his lips with an "Our Father. *Padre Nuestro, que estás en el cielo.*" I noticed he had stained his pants with urine or semen.

I couldn't help but say then, "If that man we saw this morning was a freak, this town must sure be full of them!"

That old man didn't wait for death to feel at least a moment's release from his body to be with God! But no, honey, we didn't watch it. And though Myrna gave up on criticizing, she said as long as she stayed in Mexico she never wanted to go near any more churches. (I knew there were so many that would be hard to do.)

The next day we went to Monte Albán where all we saw was a bunch of hikers, and a lot of black pottery, and a blue sky, a pure true blue. *Cielo.* The same as the word for Heaven. (We did seem near.)

I never did tell Elizabeth this story. She was too young for me to tell her. I would have told her if I could have seen her when she was thirty or thirty-five. But she left my life — that is, my life of seeing her — before that. She was always in my heart.

What then, did I tell her? Only that there were people everywhere who were friendly and nice and fun to be with.

"Don't listen to the Bells," I told her, "who are just suspicious."

Once in awhile, I'll admit, I got in trouble by not being suspicious enough. Mammy didn't bring me up to be any judge of men. She told me nothing. And Papa J wasn't much around. And when he was, as silent on this subject as on all others, a steady father to us and let us know he cared, hugged us all a lot (strange, I learned, for a Presbyterian), but a silent man.

"Aunt Rena," Elizabeth said, "you get into trouble by being too friendly."

"You will have better sense than your Aunt Rena," I told her. "All the same, she knows some things. So listen to what she's now telling you."

I said all this the Christmas the Bells had the big ruckus. Just after Ellen sickened with the cancer with Bo drinking hard. After Daddy had died. Elizabeth's mother and her husband, Bud, were home for Christmas, so I let them have the garage apartment and took the little empty half room on the other side of Ellen's and could hear her constant moaning. (I believe it had been a dressing room, not much in it, but it had a day bed.)

Bud thought his job was in jeopardy — I heard him talking about it to Bo out in the yard — so he was drinking hard, too.

And he began screaming at Elizabeth's mother who had nagged him about not looking for other work, so that I thought that he might hit her — he did that once later on, darlin', hit her hard and his Masonic ring left a mark on her cheek. And then Bo said bad things to him.

Bo said, "You never really have supported my sister."

So that Bud swung at Bo and raised his fist.

"You sissy pissant," he shouted. "Come outside and I'll let you have it."

This was Christmas Eve and we were all of us — Ellen (who was just beginning to sicken with her cancer), Bo, Bud, Leona (Elizabeth's mother), Elizabeth and me — out on the sun porch sitting around the still undecorated Christmas tree. Bo always did wait until the last minute to buy one; he was a fastidious housekeeper and hated the mess. At Elizabeth's bidding we had gathered to string the tree with lights and put the ornaments on. But Bo and Bud had been drinking since mid-afternoon and Bud and Leona quarreling, so for tree decorating, it was not the best time.

Bo didn't answer Bud when he challenged him, not at first. Only trembled. But then he said, "You're uncouth."

And Bud doubled his fist again and said, "Come outside, Buster," jerking his head in the direction of the back door. "Let's see what you're made of away from all these women."

And Bo said, "I think you better get out of my house."

And Leona jumped between them, ready I think to slap either or both. (She had a temper, honey, and was never scared of — in fact, welcomed — a fight.) Elizabeth sat at the foot of the Christmas tree, a silent onlooker, as she so often was (but I could hear her crying in the night, darlin'), and from her easy chair Ellen Bell held her stomach and moaned.

"Everybody, stop it," I said. "We've come here to trim the tree and I think we had better get to it. You men have had too much to drink."

Bud brought his fists down on the flimsy card table, piled high with tinsel and boxes of shiny glass balls, most of which spilled over on the floor, but which by some miracle didn't break, and then he walked out the door. (The next day he called in drunk from some bar and told Leona he had found a woman to be with who liked him the way he was and didn't have a family.) You can imagine what a nice time everyone had trimming the tree after that!

And what a happy Christmas dinner, with Ellen moaning from the bedroom, Leona red-eyed and silent, and Bo, Elizabeth and I pretty quiet, too. Though I tried for Elizabeth's sake to make some cheerful conversation — it seemed to me none of the full adults had behaved very well — and suggested that after dinner we all go for a ride.

"I'll bet the water front is pretty today." We had beautiful weather, 75 degrees, blue-skied and sunny. "And they say at night the yachts down in the basin are all strung with lights. Has anyone seen them yet?"

Elizabeth said she had, but that she would like to see them again. No one else answered.

"Well, honey," I continued, "after we've eaten our fruitcake, and done the dishes, why don't we just get in the car and go. Before you know it, the sun will be going down."

That was the evening that Elizabeth told me that she couldn't wait to finish high school and go on to college.

"When that time comes," she said, "I can finally leave this house."

She would leave more than that, of course, and would be gone for good. I knew I was going to miss her (though I didn't realize it fully until I saw her a few years later in Kress's, a red birthstone on her finger, with her friend, Bartola, illuminated in an eerie way under the fluorescent lights). But I also knew she would remember her Aunt Rena.

I thought about Elizabeth as I sat there at a stranger's funeral. (Well, he had been a stranger when I came in. Now he was just Joe.) Suddenly, I was so homesick for her I missed our conversations. I hadn't seen her in years. I didn't think she had ever married. In high school as I have told you, she liked a little dark-haired boy, but wouldn't much go out with him even though he seemed crazy about her. That was the problem, I think — the intensity of it scared her. She thought she might never get out of Texas and, honey, although I believe she liked Corpus Christi in lots of ways, she was ready to go.

That day in The Good Shepherd, nearly forty years after the time I remembered, my thoughts drifted like this and on and on. I don't know what went on much toward the end of the service. But I saw the people lined up to go to the altar rail and take Communion. I had cooled off and didn't anymore hear my own heart beating. Air conditioning and the flood of memories helped me. (Since early morning at the seawall I had reviewed my life.) This stopping place had restored me and given me direction. I would walk with the others up to the altar and take wafer and wine, and then exit. Just make my way through the side door. I knew when I left the church I would somehow find my way to the old house out on Palm Drive.

The Cut

Part Two

Palm Drive

After I took the sacrament, I made my way out a side door, then walked to the corner and crossed the street to the vestry, not yet crowded since the service was still going on, and used the phone to call a taxi to take me back over to Leopard where I thought I could get a bus that would take me to the back of town where we all used to live on Palm Drive.

When I left the church that same boy who first sat me down in The Good Shepherd took my arm to help me down the steps and said, "Good afternoon to you, Mother. Glad you could come."

I realized then he thought I was a nun. I just smiled and said, "Sure enough, honey." (I didn't see a reason why I should tell him any different. He was just a baby, only twelve or thirteen.)

But I never set out to be an impostor, and I hoped the taxi would come to get me out of the sight of any who had the wrong impression, and out of the heat.

On Palm Drive it would be even hotter. The street ran through a place where you couldn't hear the lapping of bay water and where, unless the town was struck by hurricane, and it was sometimes, the wind seldom blew. Ellen Bell, when she lived there, dipped sheets in ice water and strung them on a clothesline which she ran wall to wall in a back room in front of four or five big fans, kept all the fans running and the double doors to the dining room open so that the cool would blow right through.

When the taxi came and I told the driver where I wanted to go after getting a bus at Leopard, he said he didn't think I could because "The Cut" went through it.

"Well, what is that?" I asked him.

"The freeway," he said, "the interstate to San Antonio. What was the number of the house you wanted?"

Well, darlin', I didn't know the number. But if I remembered right, it was in the twelve hundred block. Or the thirteen. Which is what I told him.

"I used to get off the city bus at Leopard and Palm," I said, "and after I walked a block or two I was at the right house."

When he asked how long ago this was, I was embarrassed to tell him. He said the only way I could get to that house on this day was over the freeway pass after climbing up a bunch of stairs.

"Honey," I told him, "I don't think I could do that on a cool afternoon, let alone on this one. So maybe you had better take me and let me off at Noakes."

I remember Noakes as being lined with pin oaks, the street Elizabeth came home on after returning from a day in school. I always admired the yards on it when I walked to meet her or walked to the IGA store to get vegetables for Ellen Bell's lunch. I thought I might like to walk to the house from that store before I realized the place was probably gone.

As I was considering this, the driver asked me if I was visiting someone. I said no, that I was just sightseeing.

That gave him a good laugh. By this time we were ready to turn onto Palm Drive. "Here?" he asked. "You want to sightsee here?"

"I used to live here," I told him. I saw right away that anymore the neighborhood wasn't nice.

When he asked me how I was going to get back, I said I would call him, that I would use somebody's phone.

"Do you know anyone here?"

"Not yet," I told him. "But, honey, I'm going to knock on some doors, so I'm sure to know someone soon."

Then he said he thought I should be careful. "This neighborhood is not a good place to stay long in," he told me. He went on to say "The Cut" began here.

"And what is that?" I asked him. "I thought you said it referred to the freeway."

"More like the territory the freeway gets into," he told me. "The world is not what it was."

"Well," I said, "change is natural."

"Ma'am," he said, "this place is risky."

"Why, this street looks all right to me," I told him. But when I looked out the window I could see it was really poor, run down. Some of the windows of the houses were boarded up and others just smashed through.

After the taxi driver let me out and his car pulled away, I saw other houses had bars on the windows. And a chill went through me even though it was a broiling day. I had told the taxi man to go on, that I would call him.

Maybe I shouldn't have. Maybe this was the place where the world divided.

"Why," I said aloud and seemingly to no one, for the place was deserted. "It must not be safe here." (I was always slow to get things, darlin'.) I could hear Elizabeth lecturing me then.

Although some of the houses were vacant, their yards grown up in weeds, Noakes itself was familiar. Elizabeth had come to and from school on it, running as often as not, running and singing, all the young life rising in her. When I looked down the street I seemed to see her running, the ghost of the girl she was shimmering in the two o'clock heat. (Sure enough, when I looked at my watch, that was the time.) Elizabeth, the girl child I was close to on earth, a gift from my husband's family, my Juliette being gone.

But when I looked away from that phantom, I saw all the broken windows and vacant houses and yards grown up in weeds, beer cans and bottles in the grass.

Then when I got on toward the corner, I saw the back of what I was sure must have been the old Bell house where Bo tended the chinaberry tree and the pretty willow (both gone now, honey, though I thought the stump I saw by the side of the house belonged to the chinaberry tree) and the bed of banana trees and roses where he had painted gates and porches in a bright rose shade — just a little darker than the scarf I bought at Kress's. Oh, the first spring I lived there, I bought some material that color and made myself a dress. Now there were no trees or flowers or gates or even porches.

A big, ugly box-shaped room had been tacked onto the back of the house where the old porches had been, where the glassed-in sun porch had been and an outdoor patio covered over with a grape arbor Bo had constructed and planted. The big, ugly box-shaped room covered all in my memory.

When I came round to the front of the house, I saw the lattice work over the front porch was gone, too — Bo's bougainvillea had climbed and fallen over it — and the whole house was a kind of dirty yellow, although it hadn't in years been painted any color, trimmed in an ugly brown.

Bo used to sing a song about brown and yellow. A tisket, a tasket, a brown and yellow basket. Oh, I can hear him singing it still. But if he could have seen his old house the way I saw it, he would stop singing. He had stopped by the time he got out of the house back in his day. He lost several people he cared about — a young man he cared for (but couldn't live with the way the world was then) — while he was in it and his mother and father to cancer. Enough to stop anyone's song. (Bo went to pieces after his mother died, drank himself crazy and into the state asylum. Bud signed the papers and told them to keep him there until he dried out.) I heard the people who bought the house from Bo died of cancer, too, and I wondered if the disease was in the walls.

I hesitated before I walked up the sidewalk of that bleak yard where the grass was dead and no pecan tree or gardenia bushes grow. In that awful heat with my blue dress sticking to me I could still smell the gardenia bushes from forty years before. Elizabeth said she associated their perfume with death, not to its sadness, but to the cleansing agent in it. I could still remember her saying that. "Oh, there's a cleansing agent in death, Aunt Rena."

I wondered who lived in the house now and what they knew about the neighbors or those who had been there before. But when I rang the bell no one answered. The name Cortizar — and I guess it was the name of the people who lived in the house — was on the door. Some way it made me think of the word for heart, *corazón*, and I wished I could have taken the association as a warning, read it as a sign! But I didn't and I had lost interest in finding out much about the people or going in the house. The heat was getting to me, honey. I felt dizzy. I didn't think I wanted to stay on Palm Drive long.

And I wondered why in the world had I wanted to come here?

I saw the fat, stubby palms that had lined the street were chopped down, only stubs left. (I learned later that was because of too much water during a flood, that they had grown sick from all the water, that the very elements that nourish us also kill.)

I wished then I had just stayed back on the seawall fishing. I must have been crazy to leave the waterfront where the fish were nibbling or beginning to, the breeze blowing and where Renato, that sweet boy I met at Kress's had dropped by. I wished for him. People always said Gulf breezes cooled you in Corpus Christi. Well, I can tell you they didn't reach those here.

Why had Leeland wanted me to come to Corpus Christi? For a few minutes when I was in the church I thought I knew. But I didn't anymore. What was it Leeland thought I would find?

As I turned my back on the front door and walked back down the broken sidewalk (yellow weeds in the cracks) across the burnt up front yard to the street, I saw a big, black car, a long Caddy, round the corner at the end of the block through waves of heat. I watched it come slowly closer and closer, a door bashed in and paint chipped off the back bumper. Then I saw Julio inside!

Why, how does that boy get around all over town in that great big car with no money? (I almost asked aloud.) And him hardly old enough to drive!

The dog track wasn't far away, I suddenly realized. The taxi driver had said it was just the other side of the freeway. Maybe Julio was in this neighborhood to pick someone up.

"Julio!" I called out, but the car was going past me. "Julio! It's Renato's friend, Rena!"

But the car had passed me by.

The heat beat down, down. And I knew would get worse. I was sick from it, darlin', and from being in a place that no one seemed to care for. And from the stench of gas from the nearby oil refinery. I didn't care who lived in the house or anything about the neighbors. I just wanted Renato's little brother, or somebody, to take me out of there.

"Julio!" I called again. But the car was gone.

Then a few minutes later when I rounded the corner, I saw it on Noakes Street going the other way.

Going really slow, crawling. I thought it was peculiar for a car to crawl like that. I asked myself if I was having hallucinations in the heat. Heat itself has a presence, honey. You can just about see it come at you in waves.

Scared me a little. It's only Julio, I told myself, Renato's little brother. And I should be glad I've found him. No reason at all not to flag him down. And I kept walking toward the car.

It looked like it might stop. And when I could look its driver in the eye and see that it was Julio, I spoke.

"Julio, do you remember me? Rena? Renato's friend."

He didn't have the manners Renato did, never answered me, only asked, "What are you doing out here, Mrs.?" And although he had stopped the car, he didn't invite me in.

"I used to live out here," I said. "Forty years ago with my husband's people."

He looked disbelieving, so I turned around and pointed.

"In that house right there," I said.

I wanted to add that in its way it had been beautiful then.

"The people who live there now don't seem to be at home."

When he didn't respond I said, "I'm tired, honey, and need a ride. If you could take me over to Leopard, I could get a bus from there."

He said, "I have to wait here. I have to meet somebody."

I wondered if he had been to the dog track and if with Renato's hard-earned twenty he had won any money, but I didn't bring that up. Instead, I asked, "Well, do you know anyone in the neighborhood who would let me use a phone?"

"I might," he said, and pulled what looked like a tiny telephone out of his pocket (it might have been a real phone's baby).

I had never seen anything like that before.

"Do you have a message for me?"

All at once I wondered if the dog track was what he wanted Renato's twenty for; maybe he had just needed it to gas up this big old car. Why would he ask me if I had a message?

"No, honey," I said, "should I have one?"

My own question made me wonder if Renato had told me something I had forgotten, if there was something I was supposed to pass on.

"Did Renato say I would have something to tell you?"

Julio just looked at me, disgusted.

"I shouldn't have come out here," I said to him. "I forget sometimes I'm an old lady. Is that a phone you have there, honey? A real phone? If it is" (and he had nodded that it was), "I'd be much obliged if you would use it to call a taxi."

When I said that, Julio revved the engine which made me think he was going to take off.

"Wait, Julio," I said. I couldn't believe that he was leaving. "Julio," I continued, "don't go."

I wondered if maybe he was going to let me in. I didn't have time to wonder long when I saw its side door fly open — Julio must have pushed a button for its release. And I had just taken a seat inside, mumbling, "Thank you, honey," so relieved I can't tell you that the boy had obliged me and that I was out of the worst heat, when I heard the shots. And I knew that's what they were even though the sound wasn't "bang-bang" like in old shows, but "pop-pop," and almost pretty, a soft cracking noise of the kind you hear when opening a string of shiny red and green crackers on Christmas morn.

Crack Cocaine: One

The bullet cracked the front and then the back window glass, and whizzed, or I guessed it did, past me. I saw that Julio's shirt was torn at the top of his right shoulder and that he was bleeding. (Oh, honey, the blood oozed through Julio's cotton shirt, and he was just a child!)

Then a second bullet broke the glass.

I don't know where those bullets came from. To this day I couldn't tell you. The street was empty, deserted. Not a soul stirring or anything, not a leaf, not a blade of grass (and most of the grass was dead), no one to see. Nothing in the houses or on the porches or in the yards. Mid-afternoon and the world, darlin', was empty, mean Old Sol a-blazing (the beautiful Sun Queen that Lucy and I loved as children, dead or asleep). And yet, those shots rang through.

"Julio!" I yelled. "Darlin'."

Julio gave me no answer as the car swerved around the block.

"Julio," I called again, touching his shoulder near the place where the blood oozed, "Stop the car. We have to get someone for you." Still no answer. "Julio, stop." I said again, "Let me drive, honey." I really thought I could do it. Never mind I didn't have a license. (Julio didn't have one either.) A highway patrolman in East Texas had given me a ticket the day I ran into a pick-up at the crossroads that took it away. "Julio," I yelled, "are you hurt?"

Of course he was! But still driving, the car careening this way and that, a good thing that at first there was no traffic. But the next thing I knew we were on the freeway. Going at a terrible speed and rocking this way and that, telephone wires strung out on either side of us all I could see. (The world seemed all sky.)

"Julio, where are we going?" I shouted.

What a question for me to ask him! I don't think he ever knew.

And it didn't matter because I soon saw that even if he had a destination in mind, we weren't going to get there. We hadn't been on the freeway long when I heard the sirens and I knew we would be stopped by police.

And I should have been thankful because the way Julio was driving, he would have soon killed us both. But I wasn't thankful because I knew when the police got to us, Julio would be in deep trouble. And all I could think of was that he was hurting, and just a baby who needed help, that I was being driven by a wounded child.

Corazón! I felt my own heart pounding.

Julio didn't try to out drive the police car, couldn't, darlin', just pulled over to one side and stopped. And then fell straight over on the wheel.

Blood stained the front seat, honey.

"This boy's been shot," I told the officer who didn't need me to tell him. "Call an ambulance."

As I spoke, I noticed a big gray cloud cross and cover the sun, and although we were on a freeway, nobody else much was on it and I guessed hadn't been (that was a blessing, darlin') and the world seemed still.

And the patrolman did that, called the paramedics who arrived in an ambulance, but before it came, he asked me a lot of questions about Julio, who he was, what had happened, most of which I couldn't answer. He didn't seem to understand a bit how Julio and I were connected and I didn't want to say much about Renato. At first I pretended I didn't remember his name.

"He is just a boy I know slightly," I told them. "I'm a visitor to Corpus Christi. I met his brother at one of the stores downtown."

I said I couldn't remember which one. I had come by taxi to visit the neighborhood where I once lived, I said, and I became overheated and the boy when he came along, gave me a ride.

The shots at the car came out of nowhere, I told them. We hadn't seen a soul on the street or in any of the houses. As I spoke, I saw the sky was getting darker though it was still in the middle of the afternoon. There was no wind at all — very unusual for Corpus Christi — but I wondered if it was going to rain. Changing the subject might have brought relief. And I almost asked the officer, "Do you think it will rain?"

After the paramedics had Julio on the stretcher and were ready to take him away, the officer said he had to drive me down to the police station for further questioning. Honey, he was very polite. But

I knew he would get in touch with Renato, that some identification Julio had on him would tell the police where he lived. And, anyway, Renato would have to know, would want to know.

"Renato," I said suddenly, "that's his brother's name."

At the police station I saw Renato was already there. He told me the hospital reported that Julio had been hit, not once, as I had believed, but twice, the second time on his left side, but that neither wound was critical. Julio might have to have a blood transfusion, Renato said, and that he was worried because like his mother and many in her family, from childhood Julio had a weak heart.

When the officers asked, Renato said he didn't know why Julio was on Palm Drive, but that he knew he was going to play a horse at the nearby dog track. (Later a hospital nurse found a racing ticket in his pants pocket, along with a note about it, and we learned the dog Julio bet on had come in third from last.) He said he didn't know of any drug involvement. The police suspected Julio of dealing, thought maybe he was meeting a contact. I remembered how he had asked me if I had a message for him, but I didn't say anything about that. Later I found out he was trying to get out of a promise he'd made about dealing, that he had called someone on his phone before he went to the track.

Anyway, after the police found out I didn't know much, they drove me back to the Ramada, but said they might call on me again. I saw the sky had gone black — by this time it was late afternoon — saw dark clouds over the water near the seawall and that the bay was still. I wanted to ask the officers, "Where is the wind?"

But it was one of the officers who asked me. I had been quiet and I expect he was just making conversation.

"Where in the world is the wind?" he asked. "Do you think it is going to rain?"

Crack Cocaine: Two

Before I left the police station, I had given Renato a hug. I felt like I'd known him always, and told him to stay in touch. I said I would like to visit Julio when I could in the hospital.

Once inside my room in the Ramada, I lay down on my bed right away, though it was only late afternoon. And except to get up once to get out of my clothes and go to the bathroom, I stayed in that bed, darlin', done in. And in the night dreamed of sirens, of red lights flashing and saw some out my window when I woke up, and looked out into the dark.

And it came to me that I was in a strange world, like the one that back in Nacogdoches I saw on television and that I had believed came only from the big cities like Houston and Dallas and, of course, New Orleans, and from up in Chicago or far out in California where they long ago made all the movies I like so much that took us through the Depression and the war. A world like the one I saw on TV news or read about — I could still read a little — in the paper. Guns firing out of nowhere, people hit on quiet streets! Deserted streets. Cars going crazily down the highways followed by ambulances and fire trucks and police.

All at once I was frightened. For I knew all this was not just in the big cities, and not just far away — but right here in Corpus Christi, right on the Body of Christ (which is all the world and all of us in it, darlin'), and which is not anymore just a sweet small place, a refuge sitting quietly on the water, a peaceful little town.

When I first saw it, the population came to 17,000. And back then, we all thought that for where it was in the world, that was quite a lot.

Oh, I thought it was the sweetest little town. And so did Elizabeth's mother.

"Oh, Rena, aren't you glad work brought us here?" she always asked me. Leeland and Daddy were building bridges and buildings and she was teaching music. "Isn't this the sweetest place? So quiet and pretty. Aren't you glad we came?"

And I was!

And I am when I remember.

But that night in my room at the Ramada Inn, I realized once and for all that the town was gone. And that the world I remembered was everywhere gone.

And when I saw those red lights flashing through my motel window, then heard the sirens, when they took me out of sleep, I asked myself: when Leeland sent me to Corpus Christi, was it just a dangerous world — more than ever a dangerous world, a violent world — he wanted me to find?

I turned on the television then, expecting to hear all about Julio, and maybe even about others in the same kind of trouble like him, and heard a hurricane warning instead. Angeline, the first of the season, the weather caster said. I remembered how black the sky had looked after Julio and I had careened down the highway and had been stopped by police and when a half hour later I had driven to the station with them, how dark it had been over the water and when I first looked at it, before I fell asleep on the bed, through the window. (To tell you the truth, I wasn't sure if it was really that dark or if it just seemed dark because of my frame of mind.) I remembered it being unusually still — the fierce wind seemed to have temporarily stopped blowing — and how the officer asked if I thought it was going to rain.

"Do you suppose that would cool us off?" he had asked finally, "or leave us just steaming?"

I said I thought it had to bring some relief.

But the next morning and for two mornings to come, we had no rain although the sky was still darkened. And we still had heat.

Time seemed almost to have stopped and as it did, Renato came to see me and told me that Julio's heart had failed, and that he had died.

Churches

Renato's family held the funeral in the Catholic Church, the cathedral on top of the hill; this time its doors were open and I had no trouble getting inside. (A big place, darlin', regal with its tall ceiling and scrolled chairs with velvet kneelers. To be with Julio's family, I had to walk down the central aisle a long way.) But it was a stormy morning with a fierce wind blowing, some rain already falling and a report from the taxi driver's radio that hurricane Angeline which everyone hoped would play itself out in the Gulf, and had been hundreds of miles from us, was gathering momentum and heading directly for our coast. I guessed that news of the storm had delayed Searcy on his way to Corpus Christi and I hoped that he was safe.

I had called Searcy right after Renato visited and told him most of what had happened, and darlin', he was upset, told me he had always thought the trip back to Corpus Christi on the bus was a crazy idea, that I had no business being there alone and that he was coming to get me. I asked him to hold off for a day or two.

"Honey," I said, "if you insist on making the drive, I'll be delighted to see you. (I would be fine on a bus, I had told him.) But you need to wait until after the funeral." (I also thought that might be after the storm.) I said I had no idea why I had come to Corpus Christi in the first place, but I had become friendly with Renato who had helped me and who I liked, and I felt obliged to stay for the funeral of his baby brother.

One thing seemed sure — this trip featured funerals. And for this one, storm warning or no, Renato's relatives had come from far and near. If there was anything good about Julio being shot — and, darlin', I have learned that most suffering, bad as it is, brings some blessing — those who came together may have been it. The death of this boy brought his family back together; his sister and her children and even many cousins, once and twice removed, children of Renato's dead parents' brothers and sisters. Everybody, or almost (at least those who lived in Texas) except Reynaldo, and nobody knew where he was. The priest told all of us who were there that the church was that morning honoring the wish of family members to say something about and for Julio since most had just arrived and hadn't been at the wake, to begin. So before the Mass proper, each member who wished to say something ascended the steps to the pulpit and spoke.

And from that pulpit which, high up as it was, seemed made for kings and queens, Jesus, as head of the family, introduced each one. Only one brother, he said, was missing, Renato's twin.

"If anyone here knows anything of our brother, Reynaldo," Jesus said, "please tell one of us. He left us years ago after our mother passed away. He grieved for her, as we all did, and maybe believed in a young man's way, that he would somehow find her again in another place. Or at least lose his grief."

(I thought then of how I had gone looking for Johnny after my baby died and I was trying to get over that and over losing Lucy. Johnny was the one person I thought I could talk to.)

This was the first time I had seen Jesus, the brother who had worked his way through teacher's college and become a teacher of little children. And he was, like I had always imagined the man he was named after, craggy faced — I often think of Mexicans as having smooth faces but, of course, not all do and besides, Jesus was half Italian — with a furrowed brow and fierce eyes (a passion burning through them, honey), but soft-spoken. In an odd way, a beautiful man. A serenity about him although he burned with life.

"And he may have lost that sorrow, or some of it, but he left us with more. And now that our youngest brother is with God, we call for word of Reynaldo again, and pray for both our brothers and offer thanksgiving for their lives."

That put me back on the train I rode into Mexico when I went off, down the coast on a bus and then onto that train at Laredo when I was only nineteen years old and already a mourner. I had spent almost every penny my cousins gave me, and some more I earned in a dress shop, on train fare, didn't stay anywhere, just spent weeks riding all over Mexico on a rickety train. I remembered someone at the Laredo station had called the one I took to Monterrey "The Silver Bullet." The first class trains were all called "bullets" because they were supposed to move with the speed of gunfire.

100

But this one hardly did, was slow and ugly, scarred paint on the cars inside and out.

My cousins back in Louisiana had spoken about Mexico as "a different world," and with my face pressed to the glass, I kept looking for it. Disappointed to see the same world, the same old world, with nothing different at all. The train was hot and noisy with babies crying, and everybody speaking fast, all that Tex-Mex Spanish ("Spic," Ellen called it). That was the same as in South Texas, but there, you heard some English, too. Maybe, I considered, I was, after all, going into a foreign place and that I would see it was foreign further on.

At the first little town where it stopped, I decided to get off since the ticket taker who did speak a little English indicated to me we would be there for awhile and I was curious about what was for sale. Through the window I could see a half dozen vendors holding up their wares, an old man with sacks of what I found out were peanuts, several women with plates of food (fried chicken and fish), another with flowers and there were little children, too, holding up sticks of gum and candy.

When I got off and stepped to the ground, an old woman came toward me with herbs and another with a blanket. Maybe they thought I looked cold or sick. Or maybe they just thought I looked like a person with enough money to be a buyer. I could see they were poor, darlin', and I thought if I bought a few things I might help them a little though I was poor enough myself. I told myself I should get something like one of the handmade necklaces one of the women showed me that would last awhile and bring pleasure to someone. I thought about Mammy then. She liked jewelry. I knew she worried about me. I gave the woman the pesos she asked for and took a necklace from her with blue stones. I would mail it from Monterrey along with a card.

When I got back on the train and began to study it, the vendors came on selling food, sugar cane, tequila and fruit, but, hungry as I was and thirsty, I was afraid it might make me sick and I also thought I should, for awhile, hang on to my money. But then a light-skinned, sandy-haired man got on and offered me a tin of juice, pink grapefruit, he said, and sweet, from the Texas valley and I took it and thanked him, grateful to have my thirst quenched and for his presence (I needed someone to speak to, darlin'), as the train rattled along and he sat next to me. I had not learned Spanish, honey, and when I got on this train it hit me that unless I saw more Anglos, I might never be able to speak.

Right away I introduced myself, explaining that I was traveling in Mexico for the first time.

"All by yourself?" he asked.

Yes, I said, but added that I hoped to find my brother in Monterrey. My brother had left Louisiana for South Texas, I explained, and South Texas for Mexico where he had gone in the interior. I hoped I would have news of him at one of the hotels in Monterrey.

"What is his name?" the man asked, interested.

"Johnny," I said, "Johnny Brock."

He pulled a wallet out of his pocket then, and took a card out of it and handed it to me.

"Ask about him there," he said, pointing to the name on the card. "Tell them Ray sent you. And good luck."

Then he put his face into the Laredo newspaper and didn't take it out until just before he got off at a little place where when I looked out the window I saw more vendors. After I realized we were going to be there for awhile, I got off the train to buy some candy from ragged children (I was starvin, darlin', but afraid to eat a piece of their mother's fish) but by the time I did, Ray had disappeared up the road.

Club Fantástico was what the card he had given me said, a spectacular nightclub I was told when I arrived in Monterrey, with tropical birds and trained zoo animals.

I didn't get there until the next day because our train broke down that night, stranding us in a desert-like place under a bright dome, a whole big sky full of stars. As I looked out the window, I thought of Mary M.

Earth Mother, I thought. Star Mother.

Before this, the silence of the night had come to me through the window even though the wheels on the rails were making a lot of noise. Everything was dark except for the big moon centered in the window and circling it, or seeming to, the stars.

I drifted into sleep with a sense of peace, honey, and I guess it was hours later when the big bang woke me up. I was scared until I realized the noise came from the brake. Why were we stopping in the middle of the desert? We never found out, but a few hours later we were going again.

During this time everyone was awake and told stories of their lives, and I thought of Johnny and how he used to introduce Lucy and me.

"Lucy who stays at home and helps us all so much, and Rena who gallivants and visits with all the people."

Then to make me feel better he would grin and say, "She's like me that way, I guess."

While we talked of our lives and laughing and joking (that made us less afraid), a man took out his guitar and we all sang "*Cielito Lindo.*" I was singing as the sun came up and I never forgot the colors I saw in the sky or the green land, for we were in, by that time, a green place.

Jesus spoke of Julio's childhood, how Julio seemed to lose his speech after their mother died.

"We all grieved, but he who was her baby, especially. We hope he is with her now."

Renato got up then and said he had discovered his brother had written a note asking someone to count him out of a transaction that was to take place near the corner of Noakes and Palm Drive, that he had a good tip on a dog, a 20 to 1 shot, and he had saved and collected more than a hundred dollars to bet. (Honey, the dog's name was Angie — can you believe that? — nearly the same name as the hurricane whirling toward us from out in the Gulf.) The note Renato found in Julio's pocket said he had called and left a message, but he thought he had better also write to explain "why I don't anymore need this job."

Of course, he never mailed it — Renato couldn't find any envelope or address — but the telephone call got his message across. Renato's voice was close to breaking.

"He had never been mixed up in anything bad," Renato explained. "He was never a gang member. I don't believe he even knew much about gangs. If he had, he would have behaved differently. He would have been scared.

"He was a naive boy. If he wanted fast money, it was to help his family, for he worried for all of us, and if he got mixed up with gangs near his end, it was because he was so discouraged. He had been like that — more discouraged than the rest of us — since our mother's death."

Tears streamed down my face as he spoke. Johnny had wanted fast money, not just for himself, but I felt sure, to help his family, too. Before he left he often said he wanted to help us all. He had been running drugs, darlin' (though in those days, it was mostly marijuana).

All this came back to me as I heard about how Julio thought he would win big money on a dog. Renato said someone who hung out at the track and wanted to sell him a ticket probably made up this story. And that Julio thought he could use this money to help put food on the table and to pay his own way through the summer. When it came to spending money, sometimes he made errors in judgment. What fifteen-year-old doesn't?

Before he talked with anyone else in the family, he had lied about his age and agreed in writing to pay off a gas-eating old car (Jesus and Renato had just found out) and a cellular phone to go with it, and he hadn't had his learner's permit to drive long.

In the past years he had always had a job at the CALLER TIMES. This year the paper cut its staff, even cut those who worked in circulation. Julio hadn't known where else to get a job — he had never been good with fixing cars — if he had more sense about him, he would never have bought the one he drove — and he couldn't make anything much by working in yards (too many people were doing their own yard work or letting them go) and none of the stores were hiring, so he thought of the track as a place to make some fast money. Even if it had been, he thought of it too late. For he also had an idea about something else before (something more dangerous) or, more likely, met someone somewhere who had an idea about it for him. But he had no history of being mixed up in gangs or drugs, had been a home loving boy, and a happy little boy who liked to play ball and sing songs. Only after their mother had died — and she, too, had been taken from them because of a weak heart — had he become unhappy.

When Renato sat down, Mara rose to say that after they lost their mother, she had tried to be the mother of the family, and that she had felt responsible for Julio, especially, but taken special pleasure in him, too.

"He was a happy boy who enjoyed life!" She told everyone how he enjoyed his meals (he was a chunky boy, darlin') and how she liked to cook for him though she was just fourteen and not much more than a child herself, and how he liked to sing songs when Jesus, who was musical, played the guitar. And how he enjoyed the neighbor children and played ball, kicked around a ball with a bunch of Mexican boys who lived nearby, after supper.

But not too long after her *quinceañera* which her brothers gave her, although it cost their hard earned money, she met a young man who courted her and before she was seventeen, left the family and Corpus Christi for San Antonio to begin a family herself. And now she was a mother with her own children. They sat beside her, darlin', three pretty little girls no more than a few years apart, the youngest just a toddler, in fancy black net dresses, and pieces of black net pinned to their dark heads. (Mara wore black, too, with a black lace shawl over her head.)

As she spoke, I remembered from Mammy's naming book and also from Leeland's readings from the Bible that Mara's name meant "bitter." But she was not bitter though she had every reason to be. Something saving in her kept her this side of rancor, kept her speaking sweet.

That speaking somehow brought back Monterrey and the nightspot where I got the only news I ever had of Johnny after he ran away into Mexico and left the rest of us without any word.

And outside I could hear the wind blowing. The first thing the priest had said after we entered the church was that reports indicated Corpus Christi might have gale force winds by noon, and for the safety of all of us mourners, the speakers would keep their remarks, and he the rest of the service, brief. And Jesus, when he rose, said he would speak for only a short time about his beloved little brother. That Julio would have wanted all of us who mourned him safe.

Then I thought again of Searcy and hoped he was all right. I knew he hoped to take me to the church. He said he would try to arrive in Corpus Christi before mid-morning. But he hadn't showed up, darlin', so I left a message for him at the Ramada Inn and took a taxi to the church. I thought we would probably have to head inland after he got here, maybe drive all the way to San Antone. Outside the cathedral, the wind made an eerie sound.

When I remembered Club Fantastico, I knew what Mara was feeling for her brother. For it was there in that strange supper club that I learned our own beloved Johnny had become a runner for drugs. (I somehow thought that might be true when I heard whispered talk about marijuana "pick ups" back in the Laredo station.) Although I had not been to a nightclub anywhere when I arrived there, the Fantastico was not like any I had imagined. In the first place, only a little of it was indoors — most of the place was garden, walled in, with monkeys and jungle birds in cages, and some other birds, along with a group of peacocks, just wandering or flying around.

When I entered the front door of that place and walked for the first time across the bar room that opened onto the fantastic park with its animals and even what looked like a couple of trapeze performers walking around in costume, I can tell you I heard my heart beat. My mouth went dry when I entered and it was hard for me to speak.

But when a waiter came over to me and asked me if I was meeting someone (he spoke in English when he saw I couldn't answer in Spanish), I shook my head no, then handed him the card the man had given me on the train. Then I told him, "The man who gave me this said you might have news here of my brother, Johnny Brock."

The waiter left me then and returned with a sandy-haired man, who looked and spoke like a Texan, and who guided me through the room and out the glass doors to the full expanse of lawn and seated me at a table.

He said, "What can I do for you, honey?"

I told him the man, Ray, who I met on the train, had said someone in the Fantastico might have news of my brother, Johnny Brock, who had disappeared several years ago.

Yes, he said, he knew Ray. Ray had been an employee of the club, but he didn't know Johnny.

"I'm sorry, hon, but I don't know anything about your brother. I'm afraid Ray sent you to the wrong place."

When I showed him letters Johnny had written to me, he just shook his head.

"I'm sorry, sweetheart," he said.

Then he asked me if I was also looking for a job. No, I told him, only for my brother.

"I'm sorry," he said, "I don't know what happened to your brother."

But something about the way he said it, or maybe it was just his expression, made me think he did. Then he asked if my husband was with me, and I said I had no husband. (No, darlin', it wasn't a smart thing to say.)

"Oh, then, is your mother or father with you?" And I shook my head.

He walked me down the hill then and seated me at a table, and told me he would bring me a menu and that he wanted me to order anything I liked and that my dinner would be on the house.

He said, "Honey, after your long trip you must be starved."

Then he disappeared and in a few minutes, a waiter brought me a large gold menu with *Club Fantástico* scrawled across the front, and another man, a good looking Mexican, sat down beside me, and made some smooth conversation, telling me I looked like I should be on the American stage — this was before the movies had taken hold — then moved his chair in closer and closer to mine, and asked the orchestra which was nearby to play what I can only say was a wild song and the next thing I knew that man's hand cupped my breast.

And all through this time, the peacocks were screaming and an aerial artist was running back and forth on the high wire which had been set up down the hill. And I was getting dizzy from watching him and from a foamy drink! And I supposed I had, after all, found what people I had talked to said they came to Mexico for: a different world.

But it was chaos, darling. Behind the pretty name of that nightclub spangled across the front of it in gold letters, I found myself in a place of chaos where nothing made any sense.

All this came back to me in an instant as Mara told about her love for her baby brother, and as I heard the eerie wind whistling outside.

And then the priest say:

"Padre Nuestro, que estás en el cielo, santicifado sea tu nombre."

In no time at all I was once again taking wafer and wine, for as we listened to the wind, the priest hurried through the Mass.

And I left the church that stormy day in Corpus Christi, grateful for my escape through a garden wall from Club Fantastico sixty years before. As I ran I heard that pimp screaming at me that my brother had been a drug runner. "He was a no good runner. I expect he's dead by now."

All that long time ago I had been lucky to make my way back to the train and to ride all the way to Veracruz where I thought I saw Johnny making his way down a hill to the sea.

Later after riding a long ways on a train that traveled west, in Guadalajara where I got off for a day or two, I saw a flower seller somehow wear his face. And then in Manzanillo, a mask-maker who wanted to sell me one of his creations picked a mask up from his counter and held it in front of him and I screamed because for just a minute, the face I saw was Johnny's! I decided then I might be a little crazy and that I should go home. (I would have had to anyway for I had only enough pesos to ride the train back across the country and into Texas, where I hoped to get another train up the coast into Louisiana with the ten dollar bill still left in my bag.)

And I did, darlin', and Mammy, when she saw me, wept and wept.

108

"You are so skinny," she said over and over as she brimmed my plate with garden vegetables and chicken fricassee, and later, wearing the necklace with blue stones I had sent her, spooned up a bowl full of berry cobbler for my dessert. She thought that not just Johnny and Lucy, but that all of her children might be dead. And to tell you the truth, I felt like I very nearly was. I had hardly eaten in weeks.

All this came back and yet was leaving me as I moved toward the center aisle in that cathedral in Corpus Christi where I attended Julio's funeral and took the Sacrament at the end of a High Mass.

I bumped into Renato then and felt his arm go round me. He brought me back to myself and felt so good to me, darlin'. And I knew why I was there. This boy and I were linked.

I didn't understand the reason for it — could hear Leeland saying, when I asked why he and I were together, "There's no reason, it just is." I guess life's not what they call a linear equation or maybe any other kind — I was never good at mathematics, darlin', or in translating languages, or even learning them. Or in science class. I didn't know why — and maybe there was no why — but he might have been my own child, or Lucy's or Johnny's. I felt as close to him also as I always had to Searcy who long ago came into my life. And who I hoped was still safe.

I wondered where Searcy was.

But didn't wonder long for we had no sooner walked through the cathedral's big front doors when I saw him at the bottom of the steps.

"Searcy," I called as I stepped into the wind — and rain, too, darlin', for it had begun to fall — still holding onto Renato.

"Searcy," I called again and saw him wave.

In a parked car I also saw the stranger (a handkerchief tied around his face, and yet the part that showed eyes and forehead looked familiar), but I hadn't any time to think who this was. The idea that something was not right about me seeing that man in the car did go through my head, but mostly I was concentrating on telling Searcy that we had to get out of Corpus Christi, and I was going to ask Renato if he or any in his family needed a ride. (Oh, but darlin', they still had the cemetery to get to.) But I didn't get the question out. I saw that the man in the car somehow made the same shape as Renato, for all the world looked like Renato, could have been Renato if Renato had not been right beside me, holding me under one arm.

And then in an instant I heard the pop through the weird sound the wind was making, and the splashing sound the rain was making, the pop through all of that, through the wet plopping and the whooo, whooo, whooo.

And in that same instant felt myself falling (into some terrible pain, darlin'.) Was Renato falling, too?

Oh, it's hard to tell you how it was.

But fantastic as it sounds — in my life this church had become a Club Fantastico Number Two — the wind finally had me. And sucked me into its vortex, a dark funnel.

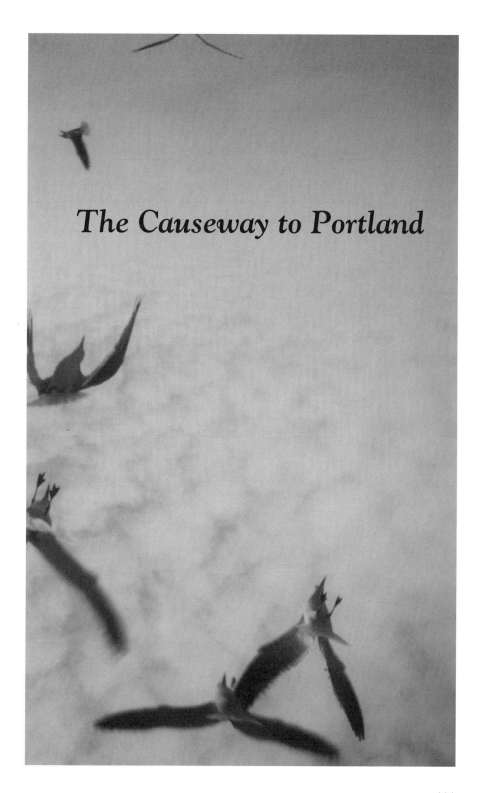

The Causeway to Portland

The Causeway to Portland

Was it my own death? Was that what Leeland had sent me to find?

If he had, I didn't recognize it.

Just fell into the wind (and for awhile into pain, darlin'), then mostly into the SOUND the wind was making, a hmmmmm, hmmmmm, hmmmmm, at first, then more distinct: an au ooo mm; then louder, AU OOO MM, AU OOO MM, a grimness to that grinding noise. And that scared me.

(But once I got past it — or, maybe just into it, through to its center — dying wasn't bad.)

Oh, what is happening to me, I wondered. I didn't see Searcy anymore or the car or the street or Renato, didn't know anymore if Renato was beside me. I was lost in the awful noise and in blackness.

And I had no idea where, or even who, I was.

Rena Bell Dubuffet. Who are you? That was the question the wind had always been asking.

And now I asked it, too. (Or asked most of it. I couldn't remember my name.)

And had no answer. Only again the question over and over again.

And then though I was still lost in blackness and the relentless grinding noise (that would not stop) and into what seemed like some terrible disorder, I sensed — don't ask me how — that I was on or near the Harbor Bridge over the ship basin that connected the Causeway to Portland and that soon I would be able to see just where.

On the bridge, darlin'. Crossing over. Was it still a drawbridge? (I didn't think so.) How many times when I lived in Corpus Christi had we been caught on one side or the other with the bridge up and boats passing under, waiting for whole half hour stretches and feeling our lives slipping away, in un-airconditioned cars?

I looked down through the sheets of rain that were gusting across the place where I stood, and which were whipping me hard, at the ships being rocked in their basin and then up toward the Causeway on the other side. And to one side of it the shiny building with all the Texas fishes who I guessed must be still chasing and calling to one another and some eating one another, but who at least didn't have to worry about the dark, who were either equipped to see in it if they had to or didn't need sight.

I had a hard time making my way to that highway, along the railing nearest North Beach and Corpus Christi Bay, and past the gleaming house with the Gulf fishes — and no, darlin', no cars and no one was a comin' — I would have welcomed them if they had! — feeling for all the world like Mary M. fighting the fierce wind and the rain. And after a long time of walking — oh, my walk of a few days before past all the churches on the hill had been short by comparison (but good practice), seeing someone who looked like Jesus (the Jesus in the Bible, darlin') or the way I thought of Him, before me, smiling at me, and more and more resembling Renato's older brother, then fading away into the storm. No sign that would stop; the rain was really coming down. And big waves kept breaking right over the road.

And I thought, why, after all, Heaven may be lateral. And our world, even those parts below sea level, God's body, not a way station that we just pass through on our way somewhere — our world all broken and bruised and scarred from abuse, but not just a stop on our route, not a place we can wreck and abandon.

But our eternal home.

It came to me then that with all the suffering in the world God must suffer most, that whatever happens to us must happen to God, too. (God, a word, darling and, yes, The Word, but part of us and living — A He-She-It — we are never separated from.)

As I found myself on that highway with rain pounding and the wind whipping me (but me somehow being able to stand it), I thought, why Heaven is not some distant place but right here. No more foreign than Mexico had been to me when I went there as a girl (looking for another world and, except for Club Fantastico, finding the same old one).

I worried I might never get down that highway. I walked and walked, all bent over, holding onto the railing and soaked clear through and didn't seem to get very far. And wondered how I was

114

able to move at all. I didn't know what had happened, or where I was walking or what for.

It was a hard passage, honey. And to tell you the truth, I was about ready to give up on it and maybe would have if I had known how to do that, but I saw, or thought I saw, through the gusts of rain and wind a shed of some kind a little way down the road and way beyond that I seemed to see a light.

(I thought then of Johnny, of Lucy and I running after him and of the fireflies we all wanted to trap in our jars.)

And I told myself, well, maybe I can reach that, the shed anyway, which would give me some shelter and would maybe even have a bench in it where I could for awhile sit down. If I could rest myself for a time and dry out a little, I might then be able to think of what next to do.

I hadn't considered this long when I seemed to see Bo Bell coming toward me, crossing over toward me from the other side, the Nueces Bay side of the road, waving and calling and, honey, he was the last person in all the world (or beyond it) that I was looking for.

Bo had died, I knew some years before, for Searcy told me he had a letter from Leona — Elizabeth's mother, Bo's sister — who had cared for him during his last years of heart attack and stroke, and who lived nearby — in a town nearby — though we never visited. (And I wonder now why not.)

Anyway, I thought I saw Bo — waving and crossing the Causeway, and through all the wind and rain walking straight toward me — who wanted to speak of his life.

Bo had cared for a shy young woman who everybody thought he might one day marry — and who he even planned to marry but never did though they once had a date set at the Methodist church. He liked her, darlin', loved her in his way, and would have liked to have had his own home with a wife and children like other people. But he couldn't go through with the wedding ceremony.

As I may have told you, he cared for a young man, too. A person who brought light to his life and a kind of magic and was the one he most wanted. But couldn't have in that time and place. (Not and be accepted by his family. Not and keep his job.) And after Ellen Bell died he just went to pieces, drank himself into a state institution —

the insane asylum, darlin'. Bud and Leona put him there after he one time in a drunken rage threatened one or the other of them (and I now forget which one) with a kitchen knife.

Leona first called the Corpus Christi police who took Bo off to the city jail and after he sobered up, he requested a place to dry out. But never thought that place would be the state hospital for the mentally ill in Austin which at that time was a true crazy house. And never mind that they said he would be in the alcoholics ward, they just threw him in a room with all those poor, deranged people, and some of them had drunk too much I guess, and some were just nuts. But none of them, those who had drunk so much they had fried their brains or those whose brains were fried for other reasons, were getting any help.

By the time Bo got out, it was too late for him to do anything much except live with his sister — by then her husband, Bud, was gone. And, of course, Elizabeth, too — Elizabeth worked on her radio shows and for this station and that for National Public Radio (which none of us much heard) in many places across the country.

Well, anyway, it seemed that on the Causeway to Portland which was taking me forever to get across, in all that rain and gusting wind with waves crashing over the road nearly knocking me over and causing me, while fighting the spray from the water, to hang on hard, to the rail, I saw Bo Bell who wanted to tell me something. And as he came closer, I seemed to know what it was.

Rena, I had a sad life, he seemed to want to say. Except when I was drinking, I never had any fun. And only in the early days of that, because drinking became my torture even though that wasn't what I was after. I wanted to enjoy my life. The way you seemed to.

I wanted to tell him then there was plenty of hurt in my life, hurt and loss, loss, honey. But I couldn't seem to speak to him somehow.

Through all that storm, I saw him and was close. And yet, wasn't. Nothing made any sense.

(Oh, God, I wanted to cry out. Oh, our Father-Mother. Is it You and not Bo that I should be addressing? Or are You, somehow, one and the same?)

But for what seemed a long time, I couldn't speak at all. I was in paralysis, honey, a paralysis of the throat.

"Bo," I managed to say, finally. He had reached me and I held onto one of his arms . "Hold on to this railing with me. (Oh, honey, the wind was beating us, we were both drenched.) Tell me why it is we can withstand this and why we are here together and where we may be going?"

But he didn't answer. And that was because (I felt sure) he didn't know.

"Well, then," I told him. "What is it you want to say? Just tell me what you can."

"Rena," he said into the salt spray, into the wet dark, "I want to tell you about what I wanted. I want to talk about desire."

"Well, hold on to me, honey," I told him, "And maybe you can do it."

I pointed up the highway toward the little road side shed — yes, darlin', it was still there! "Maybe if we sit down up there, you can tell me. We can make it if we walk together. This storm may be dying down."

I made that up to comfort him and me, too, but as I spoke, the wind did seem to be subsiding some.

Walking with our arms around each other, holding each other up, so to speak, after a time we reached the shelter and yes, it had a roof and a little bench inside and cold and wet as we were (why cold I don't know because we had made our way through hot rain), it felt so good to sit there and to rest. But we hadn't done that long when Bo began his story.

(I believe we sat at a bus stop, darling, though I don't remember seeing it when I made my bus trip down from Nacogdoches and cross the Causeway into C.C.)

"I met him in San Diego when I was in the navy," Bo said. "And there, another person in my outfit was also from Corpus Christi, a man named Frank, who ran the Mexican restaurant we all went to before and after War II. Jay was a beautiful person — beautiful in almost every way, and just by being near, brought a shine to my life I never thought really existed.

"But I was too timid to get to know him well, and didn't see him again until I came back to Corpus Christi. Saw him when we went to the restaurant, Las Hadas, one Friday night to eat our dinner.

Hard to believe, but there he was, working with his paints in the hall — painting a mural. And the sight of him took my breath. I came to a dead stop there in that entry way, Mother who was in her 80s, on my arm.

'Do you remember me?' I thought maybe I blushed when I asked him. Though I probably didn't, Rena. Not with this olive skin.

"'Sure I do, Bo,' he told me and stepped down from his step ladder and took my hand. And when he did a shock surged through me. But that shock was sweet.

"He usually stuttered, you know, was a stutterer, but that day when he talked to me, didn't, not at all.

"He was living here with Frank, he said, their rooms on an upper floor. He asked if I knew Frank and I said not well. Everybody in Corpus Christi knew that Frank was queer. I couldn't very well have had anything to do with him, he was a laughing stock, the same as a freak — worse, a blight on the town! Most people whispered about him. Or pretended he didn't exist. Only the brazen laughed. Men mostly. Ha! Big men.

"I couldn't have anything to do with Frank.

"Not that I ever really wanted to. He didn't interest me much even though we had been in the navy together in San Diego where we both knew Jay.

"No, I told him. I had never really gotten to know Frank, though I liked eating at his place. Then I asked Jay to come out to the house sometime, and he said he would, and as you remember, did. What else happened during that evening I don't remember, how Mother and I got through our dinner or went home. (I was in a trance.) After we spoke Jay disappeared. But I do know from then until a long time after, life took on color and meaning and had a shape, so that I couldn't wait to get up in the mornings. And when I looked out the back windows from my bed on the sun porch at the grape arbor and the willow tree and on the other side of the walk at the flower bed with the banana trees and black roses, I saw that they all shimmered, were surrounded by a glow.

"And saw that it came from them. And when I put out my hand before me, I saw that a glow came from it, too. Saw for the first time, though I was in my forties, that the world was living. And that I was alive, too.

"I began to eat my lunch at Las Hadas every Monday. And would have gone more often if I hadn't known that would create talk.

"Do you remember, Rena? At this time the girl — Robin Lee — was in my life, a shy sad-looking mousey thing. But she cared for me and we had a good time together. And one time she surprised me by being bold. She asked me to make her my wife. And I said yes before I knew what I was doing. And I might have gone through with it. But couldn't after I met Jay and couldn't keep seeing him either. The town had begun to talk. The old bastard I worked for put me on the carpet. 'Who are his people? Where does he come from? You don't know that boy, really. I don't think you know what you are doing.'

"So, Rena, I drank myself into the insane asylum. And when I got out except for Leona — who became my keeper — I was all alone. And then lost my health.

"And now I'm here."

"Well, me too, darlin'," I said, "And if we ever warm up and get our strength here, and if this storm ever really passes we can just go on." Maybe it was because I was in the shed, but I did think the storm was dying down.

"But," he said, "I didn't finish the other part."

"Well, I guess you did," I said, "In your way."

I thought of Elizabeth then and wondered what she would tell me, or someone, when her life was over. I remembered the boy, Ben, she had cared so much for. And her friend, Bartola, whom I had met at Kress's.

Once when I lived back in East Texas and was remembering Elizabeth I thought I heard her say:

"Aunt Rena, maybe I missed love. Do you think Uncle Bo and I have that in common?"

I could hear her asking that. Hear her saying, "Uncle Bo fell in love with that young man. Jay, wasn't that his name?

"When I was in high school you know how I felt about Ben. Oh, I don't know that it was love exactly, but it was a powerful yearning. I think Uncle Bo felt that, too. Not that he ever said so, but you know when someone close to you experiences something powerful the same as, and at the same time as, you.

"Maybe I couldn't have known love until much later when it was too late, but I did have that yearning early, and who knows what it would have become? You always thought Ben and I should have just run off together.

"But I was afraid. Afraid I'd lose myself. Finally I paid a high price not to do that. Was it worth it?

"Even now I don't know. All I know is I never wanted Uncle Bo's fate. Poor Uncle Bo! A human sacrifice! For all of us. And then lost love and himself, too. I never wanted to be a martyr, didn't think in the long run I could help anyone by being a martyr. I wanted to be bold as Bartola, but couldn't be.

"And being bold like Bartola finally might not have been such a good thing. But I wish I had been a little more open, more receptive. I wish I had been more like you."

When I lived in East Texas I imagined she said all that to me.

And standing there on the Causeway I remembered hearing her with Ben one hot May night on Bo's porch, and seeing the silhouette of both of them, the scent of natural gas and gardenia in the air. And the whole porch illuminated by the bright moon, a full moon, darlin'. But because they were there together, clinging, I turned my face away, wanting to leave them to their privacy like I wanted to leave that old man in Oaxaca to his. I was in the living room where I had just turned out a light, just the other side of the front door screen. Darlin', it didn't seem right to look. I watched her hands, small but strong and agile, run up his arms, across his wide shoulders, rumple his silky blue shirt.

"Ben, Ben," I heard her moaning, and it was a sound to break the heart. And then heard him whispering something, and both of them sighing. And her crying. I think she was crying.

Hearing their sighs, and then her crying, as she pulled away and reached for the door, broke my heart. She was my child, was like my own child, anyway, and I couldn't help her.

"I have to go in now, Ben," I heard her say. "And I can't see you as often. Maybe I shouldn't see you any more."

She wasn't far from me, was just out the porch through the door — the two of them were caught in a circle of light — but even if I walked through it and went to her, I couldn't help her wrestle with her life's dilemma, couldn't help her handle the pain.

That hurt me, darlin'.

And then standing there on that bridge, my own life mostly behind me, in my mind's eye I saw Elizabeth from a distance from the seawall where she was with Bartola — a blazing August noon. She was always flooded with light, whether I remembered her in a night scene like the one I saw on the porch with Ben or on a scorching summer day. Maybe that was because what I learned from her brought me her truth: that taking what we want always has a high price. (I wanted Leeland, but look what all came with him!)

The day I saw her with Bartola was the last summer either of us was in Corpus Christi and one of the last memories I have of her when she was young. They were holding hands, swinging along the seawall together, behind them the sun burning a hole through all the world it seemed, surely through our bodies and brains as well as through the August sky. Searing heat, darlin'. Searing light. And in it I knew something.

Elizabeth, like her Uncle Bo, would be forever single. When I saw her later in the dime store (under bright fluorescent lights) talking to Bartola, who I met for the first and last time, she showed me the garnet Bartola had given her after their lunch together, from a new line Kress's carried of semi-precious stones. And when she lifted her hand for me to see it — and with the fluorescence bounding off the gem stone, it was circled with red light! I was both glad for her and filled with sorrow.

For in that artificial brightness who she was, and her fate — some now say "Karma," darlin' — was revealed.

Ellen Bell stood in front of us then — where did she come from, I wondered. I guess for a long time I didn't know because I had been looking straight at Bo who rose to scoop her in from out of the wind — which had subsided, yes, but was still blowin', darling — and draw her into our shelter and after she was inside, kept his arm around her, something, as much as he cared for her in life, he rarely did. Even odder: she put her arm around him.

"Rena, I was a block of wood," she said, looking straight at me. She looked up at Bo then. (Darlin', he was very tall — his head all but bumped the shed ceiling — and she was a little thing.) "Do you know they called us 'The Odd Couple?'"

Then Bo said, "They called Leona and me that, too."

I knew that what he was telling me was that the town thought the attachment between them, Bo and his mother, Ellen, and Bo and his sister, Leona, was too strong, unnatural, even. Incestuous was the word nobody would say. (Given the close conditions under which the Bells lived, the way in which they shut the door on others, the assumption some made wasn't hard to understand.)

I got up then so they could sit down and I walked to the edge of the shed and looked out on the Causeway, still covered with water. But the waves weren't anymore breaking over it. I looked toward Portland and I thought I saw Jesus again. Jesus from the Bible, looking for all the world like Renato's school teacher brother, but He vanished and instead I saw Lucy, just as I had for many years, and then she vanished and near the little light way up the road — oh, I was sure of it though they were just small figures — Mammy and Papa J, waving and calling to me, but then they disappeared, too — oh, darlin', this was a strange highway! — and I was wondering if I would soon see Johnny, when Julio stood before me.

Right there on the Causeway real as life. And he said, "Thank you for coming to my funeral and tell my brothers Jesus and Renato and my sister, Mara, not to grieve anymore, that I'm OK."

And I said, without asking him a single question about where he had come from or how it was he suddenly appeared, "I will if I can, darlin'. But it looks as if I won't be able to; we are on the other side of the channel from them now — see back there."

I turned toward Harbor Bridge as I spoke.

"The bridge is behind us and we are moving the other way."

(In the olden days the drawbridge would have been up.) Then I introduced Bo and Ellen Bell.

"I guess," I told him, "we were all meant to walk to Portland together."

I pointed. And as I did, I thought once again I saw my mother and father and little sister (Clarity), near the light down that way.

Scared me, darlin', somehow scared me to see them. I had seen Lucy, of course, here and there for years, but it was different seeing her here. So I turned all the way around.

122

I thought no matter what I had just said, I might get away from all these people (the Bells and Julio and my family up the road) who, after all, must be just thoughts or shadows. For as long as I could remember I had been fooled by shadows. Or maybe we were all just in a fantasy together, some sort of fantastic illusion that had come in a dream at the end of my life and sucked me in it and given me my own part to play.

For a minute I considered walking back toward Harbor Bridge to see if I couldn't get across some way back to where my life was, to the cathedral steps where I had last been and to the heart of Corpus Christi.

I looked across at the beach then, and a long way back to North Beach — and I thought I could see even in this wet, wild night, the Ferris wheel lighted and going round, and from one of the seats rocking on the very top, some people who were waving. Were they really there? It was a long way back.

How could they be? How could a Ferris wheel be running so soon after a big storm? But maybe, I reflected, it was really early in the evening, not the middle of some dark night — after all, it had still been morning when I was in the cathedral and maybe now that the worst of the storm was over, businesses had started up again and life was, as usual just going on. I would walk back to the bridge to find out, though it was far.

I wasn't sure I could make it. I had come a long way, and without Bo's help might never have reached the little shed. Even with the storm dying down I might never go all the way back again. Just thinking about it, darlin', somehow felt like defeat.

First, I decided, before I did anything else, I would go back to the shed and say good-bye to Bo and Ellen Bell.

And when I turned to do that, I looked at a young woman with my face, darlin', or anyway with a face that had some of my features.

She just smiled at me and then a bus arrived at the shed where Bo and Ellen had been sitting and without saying a word or even thinking about it, we all, Bo, Ellen, Juliette and me (yes, darlin') all got on. When we did I saw that Myrna was the driver — I was sure I was in a dream then — and her assistant, a person who asked us our names and then spoke them into a tape recorder (we gave our names

123

instead of money to pay for passage, darlin'), was none other than Billy Park! Both of them when they saw me started laughing. (Juliette and I sat right up front near them and Bo and Ellen went farther in.)

"Why," I said, "where have you been? And what brings you here?"

And asked myself, Oh! What kind of dream, what sort of strange dream, a Club Fantastico am I in?

"I always wanted to be in the driver's seat," Myrna told me, "ever since you and I went traveling together. Remember how I drove in Mexico? And now I, once again, am. Honey, I died in an automobile accident. If I had been driving I would have lived on!"

She just whooped with laughter then, and Billy, too. (They said that just a little while before they had been riding the Ferris wheel at North Beach.)

Billy told me that his death had also been connected to a mode of transportation. He had been hit by a car while crossing the street to get to the funeral parlor (to meet his mother who was making arrangements for a "family plan") and the doctors had to take off his bad leg, and during the operation he hemorrhaged and never came to.

"I guess nobody ever expected me to live long," he said.

Then he looked at me and asked, "What happened to you?"

And I told him what I suddenly knew, that I was shot by Renato's brother, Reynaldo Santos, who may have been aiming for Renato instead, who maybe thought Renato wanted his territory or had used Julio to find him so he could squeal on him to the police. One or the other. (And poor Renato didn't even know where his brother was!)

I said, "Renato was a boy I met in Kress's whose family was in trouble."

All at once I wondered what had happened to Julio, if he had got on the bus before us. I turned my head to look around.

And waved to Ellen and Bo who I could see sitting near the middle. I wondered who else was on this bus. I didn't see anybody much. But then in the back it was dark.

Juliette, who sat beside me, just smiled, and shy as I was with her, I reached over and touched her hand. I was so glad she was with me!

Then when I looked out the front window, I saw way up the road, near the grade that swooped just a little way up to Portland, little figures that somehow seemed to me to be Mammy and Papa J and Lucy, and what looked like — I didn't dare even think the name — (oh, could it be?) — All of them smiling and waving.

I was glad the bus had come (even if everything was happening too fast). Bless Myrna's heart! She had always helped me out. And I was glad to see poor Billy Park. Mostly I was glad I hadn't quit, hadn't turned back. And I relaxed a little and grew silent as we sped along.

As she drove, Myrna talked some. Told me all about those we both knew that she had recently seen, or transported. Not long ago she said she picked up an old friend of Bill Powers, a buddy from World War II, and had a good time visiting with him as they traveled across and then enjoyed catching up with Bill who helped him with his bags when he got off the bus at Portland. She thought some of Bill's family, maybe his wife, was with him and there to help, too.

"Sure enough!" I said. "I wonder if I'll get to run into him at all."

But when I looked ahead, I wondered if I was really seeing what I thought: Mammy and Papa J and Lucy — and someone else — way up the road. Maybe I was hallucinating or it was some other people. I supposed I would soon find out.

But the Causeway seemed endless, the way it never had in life, and our trip took quite awhile. When I looked out the window I saw the rain had really stopped. I guessed the wind was still blowing (didn't it always?) since our bus rocked. I seemed to see over the water bursts of sparks. (Lightning? Was it from lightning?) Then a flame that drew me into it or seemed to. I drowsed off, darlin'. Was I sleeping within the dream? Dreaming within the dream? Oh, darlin', even now I wouldn't say.

And when I woke I looked out at a sky full of white moonlight, then — was it sunlight? Or that flame again? — into the color orange. The Sun Queen? I asked myself. Lucy's old friend and mine, had she awakened? Was it morning? Was I looking straight into the Sun Queen's light?

Or was it just Lucy's? Or were Lucy and the Sun Queen one and the same?

I didn't know, darlin'. I only knew the bus had stopped and that Myrna was shaking me to — gently shaking me to — and that before I knew it, I had disembarked.

And that Papa J was hugging me and Mammy. And then Lucy, who was not any more a vision, but real. (*"Renee, before you know it we will together plant a garden!"*) And that we were all standing near a depot at the top of a hill. And that when I looked down it I saw the Causeway and Corpus Christi's shining, tall steel and glass buildings near the waterfront, on the other side. And that all the rest of wherever we were seemed to be sky. A feeling of boundlessness about it.

"Why," I said, "we are all in Portland. And I have never stopped here before. And I don't know a thing about this town."

And they all said I would get to know it (and that I would like it) before going farther on.

And, oh, I was so happy to be with them (and happy to see the morning) — Mammy and Papa J and Lucy, and Juliette who was still with me. Myrna, who waved to me, turned the bus around. But I saw all the others, except Billy Park (Julio and Bo and Ellen) had gotten off and walked away from where we were, in different directions, leaving me with blood kin, Mammy and Papa J and Lucy, and Juliette, who I didn't yet even know, though she was my very own child.

And then we all entered a bleak little cafe that sold coffee and doughnuts but was so depressing, darlin', with its down and out, or just very sleepy looking customers and its plain gray linoleum floor and stark white walls. Well, I thought, maybe it doesn't matter for, after all, we are in Portland. And as soon as we got seated at a couple of small tables, I looked up and for a moment thought I saw someone else. My brother.

But when I came close, he was gone. Why, it must have been just a shadow, I told myself. I must have only seen a shadow. One of those shadows I was always seeing. My own maybe? (I considered that.) Maybe I only saw my own shadow, I told myself. And it seemed almost funny, that kind of illusion.

I had grown excited over a phantom. But I had wanted to see

Johnny standing there.

And I sat there in the cafe, blue, thinking of what he had meant to me, my brother, and dreaming of what he would say to me if he were really there. Oh, I wondered, why wasn't it Johnny I had seen instead of some illusion? Why could I never find Johnny? Even at the portals of eternity couldn't find him, but only air?

As I sat there I fell into dreaming. Saw him before me, darting through the trees, running straight into the darkness. Lucy and me behind after him and the fireflies with our open jars.

I hardly saw those around me. My family, I think, had exited, each trekking off in a different direction, though Juliette, I seem to remember, had lingered for a little while. "I'll be with you soon, honey," I think I had told her.

The cafe we were in, darlin', was the kind of place where many in poor little towns start their day — oh, just after sun-up, honey — as early maybe as 4:30; this one sold mostly doughnuts and coffee, but some in the town I had come from and like many of the towns Leeland and I had lived in, featured eggs and grits and biscuits and gravy.

Myrna told me she and Mr. Teague had once owned and run a little doughnut shop, but it drove her crazy. She had to get up at 3 and open the place to make the batter for the doughnuts and get them in the oven by 3:30, and that by the time she was ready to enjoy her own supper in the evening and maybe a beer or two, she had all but already passed out. Now what kind of life is that, I ask you?

She told me she finally said to Mr. Teague, "I don't care if we are making money, we are never awake to spend it and we haven't got any children." So they sold the business.

A big barrel-chested, dark-haired fellow and a skinny tow-headed girl had charge of the Portland place. I wasn't hungry at all, though God knows after what I had been through I ought to have been (I think I'd been through too much, darlin'), but ordered coffee and a box of doughnuts to split with the family if I ever again saw them, though coffee was mostly what I had. And even before it came, I fell to dreaming. And later as I sat there drinking it, the shadow that had been Johnny appeared in front of me and then fleshed out and finally began to speak of its life.

He had been a runner for marijuana, it said. But that was it. He never dealt at all in anything harder. He thought he would just do it for awhile to get some money together so he could buy himself a little business — maybe farm machinery.

"That's what Lucy's boy, your namesake does," I told him. "He's made it his life. The boy I call Johnny Two."

"That a fact?" this shade of Johnny asked.

"Well, I thought I might get enough money together to try it, and that maybe I could send some to all of you."

But he said he was one time in Laredo apprehended and had to flee the Texas and later some of the Mexican police. And that afterwards he worked for a club in Monterrey where he thought he might be safe until he found out how bad it was. And the ways in which they had plans to use him and that after that he just took off after the place shut down one night and went far into the interior, then after some time had passed came north again, but no further than Cuernavaca and finally settled in a crude house near the village of Tepoztlán, where he sometimes acted as a tour guide for hikers. (By this time he could speak pretty well in Spanish.) The soil, he said, was too rocky to grow anything much. But he didn't mind, he said, since he had never been in love with farming as he was sure I knew and maybe wouldn't have even liked selling farm machinery.

He did miss the water. He had always liked to fish and he missed the Gulf.

He got along, he said, though he didn't have much and after some years passed he no longer worried that he would be found by police and then he married a village girl he liked to be with and had three children, two girls and a boy, who as far as he knew, all still lived there.

By the time he was this far along in the conversation, I realized everyone had left the cafe but Johnny and me and that although I couldn't see it outside our window, I knew the sun had risen in the sky.

"I lived peacefully, Rena," the shade of Johnny told me. "I never made money like I planned and I couldn't help any of you and had to live apart." He said that was his sorrow, but in Tepoztlán, he

128

didn't have a bad life. Everyone treated him all right and after awhile he realized he liked living there. He said he had beautiful children, the youngest a girl named Rena. "After my stories of you." Then one night, he told me, his heart stopped beating.

In my dream, as Johnny talked, I seemed to see the brilliant sky outside the little cafe and I felt such a peace coming over me — I think I may have been awake by then — and when I looked out the window saw Mammy and Papa J and the biggest surprise of all, my Juliette, returning. Though her questions broke my heart.

"Oh, Mother," she asked me later (yes, darlin', she called me "Mother"), "what did I miss? Would it have been good?"

What could I tell her? Do you suppose I was still dreaming? That I had dreams within my dreams, maybe?

And I saw the sky outside going all white, bathing all of us in it.

And when I rose and headed for the door (Johnny, or my dream of him, by this time seemed long gone) and opened it so that I could join the others, there he was. Leeland. There he stood before me. Grinning like he used to. Shy as he had always been.

"I'm glad you got here," he said.

I couldn't say a thing — but I had my arms around him — for I had begun to bawl.

Now, you may ask, was all of this a dream? All of what I have told you? Not just the part about Johnny? What was in the wind — that terrible wind and where did the terror and chaos in the wind come from? And why wasn't it all chaos and terror? Because it wasn't, darlin', awful as that terrible wind was, crazy as it was, and — eerie — there was way deep inside it, a weird sense. And something that forced us to use all of ourselves to be able to stand in it.

You may ask, what did it bring me? Or you may even ask, Rena, where are you now? Are you real, or are you just a voice in my head? You may even ask if I am your own voice maybe.

Oh, darlin', you think I have the answer to so many questions!

And I might ask you some of the very same ones. Who, you who hears me, who are you? Are you a friend or relation, or some stranger (but somebody I may like to meet)? Could one of you be Johnny? The brother I followed with an open heart? Or you, Searcy? Or Elizabeth, the second child I lost?

In Between

No, darlin', I didn't die then and couldn't from Portland go away with Leeland. But seeing him, and all the others on the road, prepared me for my actual death, which was very easy — when it came, my heart just stopped. And the life I had left, sweet, or mostly. Maybe I just don't remember the pain.

I don't know why I never did see Johnny. And still haven't, darlin'. But he lives inside of me and maybe that's the most important thing.

Maybe some of our outward connections really do get lost forever. And that we just have to accept that. Anyway, it surely seems to me that — though we have to go on looking, even in eternity some people we love, close to us as parts of ourselves and who are part of us, really, we may never be able to find.

What life was left to me I used to be with Searcy who I saw still needed me and wanted me to be near him and to get to know his new wife. She was a sensible girl, darlin', but didn't take life too seriously (together we laughed a lot), so we got along just fine.

But sweet as most of this time was, and as much as I used it to enjoy being with the only earthly family I had (I never saw Johnny Two and I didn't know where Elizabeth was), only half of me was in it. The other half even then was gone.

Had permanently crossed that Causeway, asking questions. Who am I? (Always asking, honey, always asking.) Who is Leeland? What is between us? Between me and this man I'm not finished with, who is somehow at my center, without my knowing why or being able to understand, a part of my being I need and must find.

But to get back to where I was and what I was telling you:

No sooner did my arms go round Leeland — the instant I saw his face, heard his voice — when I began to bawl. And then heard something besides my own crying: the sound that brought me to the Causeway and Portland in the first place. And I was overcome by the humming, the awful buzzing, the monotonous, singing sound which numbed me and held me prisoner.

And seemed to me louder, and with it the question: Rena Bell

Dubuffet, who are you? (Was I or was the wind asking?) And then, why don't you finish what you start? And though Leeland's face had just been in front of me, the world suddenly went black and the question that seemed almost to come out of my own voice, carried me back into the sound, by then a kind of roaring, louder and more ongoing (not nice at all, darlin,) than any other I had ever known.

So that for just a moment I understood that all the world outside me that I even in blackness remembered — the bay and the Gulf beyond it, and all the fishes and the wind, and yes, all the people — Renato Santos and all his family; Julio and the drug runners; all those who laughed and cried over Julio and prayed together for him, as well as the one who had shot him, and all those who shot each other; and all those who fish and hunt as well as those who dart past the hooks and flee from hunters — I understood that all, all of these are the same, fish and fisherman, hunter and hunted, all all the same. And also the same as what is inside of me.

In that moment I understood, saw them move through and become each other. For just an instant before I became whatever I am now (and you tell me, darlin': What am I? What are any of us? What are you?) I understood this. But some way, it seemed all too big and too scary to keep in front of me and so I came back to whoever I am — the self I walked about in all those years, surely just a fragment caught up in everything else. (What do you see, darlin'?) Came back to my own voice, too — all I am now maybe. But that could be a lot.

Maybe my voice is in your head now so that part of it is you.

Is that right, Searcy?

Is that right, Elizabeth?

To whoever hears me: You who may also hear the wind... The wind singing and singing, singing all the way through me, all the way through you, through us as we are separate, and then again each other. (That's what spring meant to me every year in Corpus Christi, the sound of the wind, seeming to be all of us, singing through me and everybody and through the Gulf and Corpus Christi Bay and onto the shore.)

Coming To

I hadn't time to answer these questions or even to think about them much (and maybe I'll just leave them to you) because before I knew it, I opened my eyes and saw that I was in a white room that had to be in a hospital somewhere, and that Searcy was sitting beside me.

Was I glad, darlin'? Yes and no. I was glad to see him and glad not to be so confused about everything — just dizzy and floating through too much that was new and too many changes — glad to feel the solidity of the bed beneath me and the table beside it and to see the chips in the paint near the door, and even the ugly grayish liquid in the bottle to one side of me that I guess was going into the rubber tube that dangled from it and was attached to my arm.

But then an awful sense of loss came back to me. And Leeland's face. Oh, where was it? And Leeland? Oh, where, oh, where had he — and all my family — Lucy and Juliette who was so new — where had Leeland and all of them gone?

Although they had vanished and although I was now not sure I had ever had a solid sense of them, they and the place I had come from were more real than this hospital room. And never mind that I had been dizzy and floating for weeks and weeks; they remained more real to me than anyone or anywhere else. For a long while, darlin', the world was a shadow, though I couldn't let on.

"Aunt Rena," I heard Searcy say and saw him smiling down at me, "Aunt Rena, it's Searcy."

I had to laugh at that. "I know it's you, honey," I said, "sure enough. But tell me, what has been going on?"

"Something good, I reckon, since you are coming to."

He told me then that I had been wounded in the shoulder and though the wound was superficial, the shock from the injury and loss of blood during the surgery had strained my heart. He said they weren't sure I was going to make it. He grinned wide then.

"Since you can speak to me I guess you have." Since he was a little boy he depended on my speaking to him, he said. "You told me the first I ever knew about my family. You explained the world."

"Oh, honey," I said, "I don't know that I can explain anything anymore. But I sure do have a lot more to tell you. And when I rest a bit I will. Seems like — for just a little while — I saw your mama."

He said he was sorry he ever got into the comfort he took from my speaking, that I probably shouldn't say any more, but just lie quietly. We saw then that the nurse was coming.

And when she said, "Why, look who is awake. How are you feeling?" I said, "A little weak, darlin'." Then I asked her the time and after she told me it was nearly noon I felt myself getting hungry and asked her if she thought I could have a little broth for lunch.

And before I knew it, the boy was there with a tray with a bowl of clear soup in it. Plain broth but I couldn't remember anything ever tasting so good.

That evening the same boy brought in a supper of toast and poached egg and the next morning a full breakfast and by afternoon I had the news that I could go home. And before I knew it Searcy drove us both through the streets and down Ocean Drive and Shoreline to the Ramada motel.

And, darlin', I saw telephone lines down and Corpus Christi as a soggy mess, so many trees broken with limbs still in some of the streets. And the place I had come from, Portland as well as the Causeway to it, seemed more real than what I saw before me in the world.

All the same, Searcy said Angeline hit Port Isabel, sparing Corpus the worst. He said he had stayed right with me in the hospital on a cot the night after my surgery, told me he had removed our things from the Ramada since it was evacuated and shut down.

Had just reopened the afternoon we arrived back there and you can believe they asked us plenty of questions — the boy at the desk and the one who walked us to our rooms — since they saw my shoulder was all bandaged and my arm in a sling. The Ramada had its own troubles; all the broken glass out front had not been cleaned up, some windows were still boarded up and most of the carpet in the lobby was water stained and some was still soaked.

On our ride in, I also noticed broken glass outside Water Street Market with its oyster bar and seafood cafe, and I figured most of the places on Shoreline were a mess. Still I saw the seafood cafe was open.

"Searcy," I said as we passed it, "do you know what I'd like before I leave this town? Some seafood, maybe even oysters. I don't believe I've had any seafood in years."

"Well," Searcy said, "I guess seafood wouldn't hurt either of us, if that's what you want. But I don't know about oysters. They may be too rich and I don't believe they are in season. But we can see how you feel this evening and ask at the Water Street Cafe if you would like to go over there for dinner."

I told him maybe I couldn't eat much, probably not oysters even if the cafe had them, that maybe this yearning was mostly in my mind, but that I would like to go.

"Do you know what else I would like?" I asked him. "I would like to ask Renato and Jesus and whoever might still be around from the Santos family to come, too."

Searcy had told me first thing that Renato was all right, that I had received the bullet that had been intended for him and that the second bullet struck the church wall — fired as the gunman (Renato's own brother, darlin') was taking off.

"Well, we can call them," Searcy said, "if they would like to come that would be all right."

"I think it would be nice," I said, "if we made a little party."

When I said that I knew just why it was I had brought along my red dress, and bought to go with it, a loud pink scarf.

The Water Street Cafe

Renato said he would be pleased to eat fish or shrimp or maybe even oysters with us at the Water Street Cafe. I told him if he could to also bring Jesus and his sister Mara and the little girls along, and anyone else he would like.

"Searcy wants to treat us," I told him when he mentioned expense, "and he has plenty of money."

Searcy groaned when he heard this, but I knew that though he wasn't a man of much means, he had enough with him to do this evening up with a little style.

Searcy and I seated ourselves by the front windows of the cafe and waited for the Santos quite a while before the sun set over the water that last evening of my life in Corpus Christi.

Renato, when he did come in, grinned when he saw me, something he hadn't done, I don't believe, in days, brokenhearted as he was about both his brothers. The only good thing was that as far as we knew, Reynaldo hadn't killed anybody, only tried, so that if he wound up in Huntsville, it wouldn't be for life.

The three of us had not been at the long table near the front of the cafe where we could look out at the water more than just a few minutes when Mara came in with the three little girls who seemed to make a rainbow (no longer in black, but in pretty colors: pink and violet and green). And with her was her brother, Jesus, and all of them embraced Searcy and me, even two of the little girls, one — the older girl in green — who was shy, and the baby in pink who was bold. And Searcy ordered cokes for the children, and for the rest of us beers and iced tea. And a platter of French fries for the children and shrimp cocktails for the grown people, and when none of us objected to this order, told the waitress after we studied the menu we would continue on from there.

Although the world still seemed to me unreal, and I watched it turn into a pastel, a tinted shadow, I was at that time glad to be more or less in it.

"To all the Santos," Searcy said, lifting his frosted mug to Jesus and Renato and Mara after the drinks came, and then to me, adding, "And to my Aunt Rena whom we almost lost."

"To Julio," I said, looking at each one of them in turn and lifting my glass of tea.

Everyone drank then; even the little girls drank their *Coca Cola*. For Julio. And maybe also for me.

"It was a sweet service," I told them. "It sent him off in good standing." Then to Searcy I said, "When my time comes I want something like it. I have a little policy that should cover a plain coffin. I don't care about music or flowers or anything fancy, just that people I care about be there. You and Johnny Two if you can get him to come, and Maurine and your Bea. (That was his wife's name, "Bea.") And Elizabeth, if you can find her."

Searcy smiled and said, "We'll put you away nice."

Everyone laughed after that.

After I ate all I could of my shrimp cocktail, I decided I wanted to try the flounder which the menu said was the catch of the day.

"Nothing like fresh Texas flounder," I told them. "A sweet-Jesus fish, I always call it." (Jesus Himself seemed in it.)

Then the Jesus who was with us ordered flounder and so did Mara and Renato. Searcy ordered fried oysters which may not have been in season, but when they came he said tasted fine. As we got into our eating, we grew quiet as if we had been through a lifetime of suppers together.

From the time I had called Renato and asked him and his family to eat with us, a temporary calm fell over the world. But as we ate and I looked out the window, I saw the palm trees were once again blowing — the Santos and all of us were quiet, so I was aware of the sipping sound from glasses and the clicking of spoons. And, all of a sudden, I seemed to hear the wind once again singing. The sound of it seemed to come right through the glass.

And I knew I was back to where I had always been and might always be, and that it was a place of perpetual beginnings.

Through the glass I heard the whooo, whooo, whooo all over again.

Rena Bell Dubuffet, the wind seemed to be singing.

Who am I? I had always wanted to ask the wind that and then to be able to answer the question. And then to ask and have an answer to: Who are you?

Who are all of you who hear me?

Is one of you Searcy? (Can you hear me, Searcy?)

Is one of you Elizabeth? (What do you have to tell me?)

And, Johnny, where ever did you go?

Oh, I keep listening, listening.

And sometimes it seems I can almost hear you and some one of you soon will tell me, that I will have another answer even as I am delivering my own. For part of you is me, and me you. Darlin', we are each other. And I can almost hear you. The wind keeps singing and singing.

I can almost hear your voice.

Eve La Salle Caram is the author of "Wintershine: A Book of Maps, Pictures, Laments, Celebrations, Praise," and "Dear Corpus Christi" and the editor of "Palm Readings: Stories From Southern California." She grew up on the South Texas coast, attended the University of Texas at Austin, received a Bachelor's degree in Literature from Bard College, studied Fiction Writing at Columbia University and holds a Master's degree in English and Writing from the University of Missouri, Columbia. She teaches Literature and Writing at California State University, Northridge, fiction writing in the Writers' Program at the University of California at Los Angeles, and has taught writing in a number of colleges and universities, including Stephens College, The University of Missouri and the University of Southern California.